ARDEA

Before you start to read this book,

take this moment to think about making a donation
to punctum books, an independent non-profit press,

@ https://punctumbooks.com/support/

If you're reading the e-book, you can click on the image below
to go directly to our donations site.
Any amount, no matter the size, is appreciated
and will help us to keep our ship of fools afloat.
Contributions from dedicated readers will also help us
to keep our commons open and to cultivate new work
that can't find a welcoming port elsewhere.

Our adventure is not possible without your support.
Vive la open-access!

Fig. 1. Hieronymus Bosch,
Ship of Fools (detail; 1490-1500).

Ardea

A Philosophical Novella

Freya Mathews

punctum books ⓟ earth, milky way

ARDEA: A PHILOSOPHICAL NOVELLA
© Freya Mathews, 2016.

First published in 2016 by
punctum books
Earth, Milky Way
http://punctumbooks.com

punctum books is an independent, open-access publish-er dedicated to radically creative modes of intellectual inquiry and writing across a whimsical para-humanities assemblage. We solicit and pimp quixotic, sagely mad engagements with textual thought-bodies. We provide shelters for intellectual vagabonds.

Cover Image: W.B. Weber, *Great White Heron* (1949), used with permission from National Geographic Creat-ive. Book design by Jake Valente.

ISBN-13: 978-0615845562
ISBN-10: 0615845568

Facing-page illustration by Heather Masciandaro.

this book is dedicated to Satao, c. 1968 – 30 May 2014

Table of Contents

The Legend of Faust
Preamble

The Faust legend derives from a chapbook, the *Faustbuch*, published in Frankfurt in 1587. Penned by an anonymous author, it tells a story based on various contemporary tales of errant magicians and alchemists. In the *Faustbuch*, these figures were presented as a single character, Johann Faust, whose pivotal act was to sell his soul to the devil in exchange for occult secrets and powers. The story was subsequently dramatized in England by Christopher Marlowe; his play, *The Tragical History of Doctor Faustus*, appeared in 1604. Marlowe's play was then absorbed back into Germany where, in many different adaptations and versions, it entered the repertoire of itinerant theatre companies and even fairground puppet shows. It was this folk tale that inspired Goethe's famous play, *Faust*, published in two Parts, the first in

1808, the second after the author's death in 1832.[1]

In Goethe's play, Faust is an eminent university scholar in early middle age who has grown disenchanted with his cloistered, excessively intellectual way of life and longs to experience the full range of human passion and power. He is a man with a modern consciousness—he has undergone the Copernican Revolution in philosophy as well as science and has the breadth of knowledge that came with the 18th century Enlightenment. But in Faust this expanded consciousness is at odds with the social and economic conditions of his provincial German world, which is still basically feudal. Faust lives in a small town in which the people exist in pious ignorance, their conditions cramped both architecturally and spiritually. Faust's mental expansion has isolated him from these people but has brought him no compensations because it is abstract: he longs to develop himself experientially to fill the expanded world of his intellect. He wants not only to know everything but to experience everything, to become everything, to actualize within the compass of his own being every human possibility. In this he embodies not only the old dream of the magus but the restless striving of the modern condition.

At the start of Part I, Faust is a reclusive scholar; by the end of Part II, he has become, literally, a property developer. He has understood that in order to actualize himself he has to re-fashion the external world—only in a world in which the old, closed feudal order has been physically and psychologically broken down will human beings be free to expand themselves to their full potential. In the demolition of the old order however, many things and people are sacrificed: whoever and whatever stands in the way of Faust's will to self-expansion is cut down.

The play opens with a Prologue in Heaven. The devil, Mephistopheles, is complaining to God about the base corruptibility of humankind. God states that there is at least one

---

[1] Michael Beddow, *Mann: Doctor Faustus* (Cambridge: Cambridge University Press, 1994).

individual, Doctor Faust, who is so upright and high-minded as to be incorruptible. Mephistopheles wagers that he could lead Faust astray; God, confident of Faust's integrity, accepts the wager.

In the first scene, Faust appears in his dingy medieval study, despairing over his lack of connection with the sources of life; indeed he is contemplating suicide. As he leafs through an old book of alchemy, he happens upon an occult symbol of the Earth Spirit, and, calling it up, idly challenges it with the arrogance of a modern consciousness. Then, in an effort to throw off dejection, he steps outside to mingle with the crowd celebrating Easter in the town. When he returns, refreshed, he is followed by a large black dog.

Indoors, the dog turns into the figure of a man whose appearance and attire are suggestive of a travelling scholar. Urbane and wry in manner, not to say downright sardonic, this is of course Mephistopheles, who has used Faust's moment of meddling with occult energies to gain entrance into the Doctor's world. As a personality, Mephistopheles is not without insight into human motives, at any rate the baser ones. Altogether he presents as not unlikeable, except on those occasions when his true underlying coldness and carelessness are revealed.

Faust and Mephistopheles strike a deal: Mephistopheles will show the disaffected scholar everything life has to offer. He will supply Faust with the means necessary—money, speed and know-how—to achieve this end, on one condition, that Faust's soul be delivered into his possession at the moment of death. Faust adds a further condition to justify the pact in his own eyes, namely that if at any moment he should become comfortable and content, inclined to give up his attitude of striving, then, in that moment, his life should end. With this condition Faust reassures himself that it is a loftier goal than mere egotism that drives the otherwise unseemly pact.

So Faust and Mephistopheles embark together on the great adventure. The first connection with the sources of life that Faust seeks is that of eros. He notices a pretty young girl in town, only fourteen years of age. Her name is Gretchen. She is innocent, modest, devout, embodying in her very person the small village world of the medieval order. Out of nostalgia for this world—the world of his own childhood—Faust becomes infatuated with Gretchen. By use of magic, the scheming Mephistopheles gives him access to the girl's little household, and soon she is in love with the apparently worldly, wealthy stranger who leaves her expensive gifts and opens up her heart and her horizons. Faust seduces Gretchen, but then retreats from the intensity of her ardour and longing. A series of personal catastrophes rapidly befalls the girl, triggered though not intended by Faust. Her brother, mother and illegitimate baby too, when it is born, are all killed, and she herself is imprisoned and executed, a victim, not only of Faust's lust and the baleful influence of Mephistopheles' interventions, but of the ignorance and prejudice of the feudal order.

Gretchen is the first sacrifice at the altar of Faust's hunger for life. Not being a callous man, Faust grieves for her, but only briefly. He is not deterred from his quest. In the second half of the play, replete with classical allusions lost on most twenty-first century readers and written decades after the first half, the plot becomes allegorical, the scene of Faust's quest opening out dramatically in time and space. Together with Mephistopheles, he roams ancient landscapes of battle, sorcery, empire and thought, inserting himself into founding dramas, contriving to marry Helen of Troy, consorting with sirens and sphinxes, conversing with philosophers, engaging in large-scale speculations on the cosmos and the human condition. Such is his ambition that he seeks to embody, or absorb into his own being, the entire sweep of Western civilization. Towards the end of Part II however, the play shifts back from allegory to Faustian psychology. Stale and sated after having pursued experience on such a grand scale, Faust is enjoying a quiet moment with Mephistopheles. He is indulging in a romantic little reverie on nature—contemplating the "towering swell" of the sea—when suddenly he becomes unaccountably angry at what he sees as its wasted power!

"There wave on wave, by hidden power heaved,
Reigns and recedes, and nothing is achieved."[2]

Reinvigorated by a sudden new horizon of aspiration, Faust conceives a plan to tame the ocean—specifically to reclaim and drain a whole coastal region and develop it into a modern housing complex where multitudes of people— refugees from the claustrophobia of the feudal order—can live free and expansive lives, all enjoying the material and social conditions necessary for further self-growth.

Faust is, in other words, beginning to appreciate that emancipation, the freedom to fulfil one's own potential, requires not only an inner commitment, such as he undertook in his transaction with Mephistopheles, but a rearrangement of external conditions. The entire material context of life has to be reorganized. With characteristic energy, Faust takes it upon himself to effect this reorganization, using the underhand, Mephistophelean means on which he has come to rely. A large labour force is deployed; labourers are driven hard. The huge coastal construction site is artificially lit at night so that work need never pause. There are many industrial deaths and accidents. Nevertheless, people come from far and wide to settle the site, and Faust is held in high regard for the opportunities he affords for a modern way of life.

Although he is finding himself more fulfilled in this large-scale economic and social enterprise than in any of his previous, more personal adventures, there remains an obstacle to Faust's ambition. At the edge of the great reclamation site is a dune that has eluded purchase. On the dune stands a grove of linden trees, and in the grove nestles a humble cottage occupied by an elderly couple, Baucis and Philomen. They exemplify all the sturdy, unromantic virtues of the pre-modern order: piety, fidelity, constancy, kinship and familiality. Faust has tried to negotiate with the old couple—he has offered them new accommodation in the housing complex—but, like

[2] Johann Wolfgang Von Goethe, *Faust: Part Two*, trans. Philip Wayne (London: Penguin, 1959), 221.

indigenous people everywhere, they are dwellers in the land, lovers of home, and they have stubbornly refused to budge. As people in the way of progress however, they have to go. Faust arranges for Mephistopheles to remove the couple forcibly, but, as usual, Mephistopheles' carelessness brings catastrophe in its train: Baucis and Philomen are not merely evicted but burned to death in their cottage.

Faust is horrified. He had not meant for Mephistopheles to murder the old couple. Thenceforth he is haunted by "care"—what we today would call depression—and afflicted with blindness. But even now his energy is not spent: relentlessly he drives himself and his workers to finish the job.

At last the housing complex is complete. The old, closed order has given way to a new, modern era. Having succeeded in his mission, Faust finally acquiesces in death. But although Mephistopheles has long since won the wager with God, he is not rewarded nor is his pact with Faust upheld. In a scene set amongst angelic choirs, Goethe, indulgent towards his hero, has Gretchen reappear to snatch up Faust's promised soul and deliver it safely to Heaven instead. Faust is redeemed—by the "love" of the long-dead child who was the first casualty of his appetite for life. Women, Goethe seems to imply, love, and by their love condone, men like Faust, even if such men ruin and betray them, because at a deeper level such hunger for life honours the life force—and hence eros—more truly than any merely moral posture can. This is the implied greatness of the Faustian life—not a moral greatness but the greatness of a destiny dedicated to the life force itself.

Goethe clearly identifies closely with his ambiguous hero—his own life was also lived with ferocious energy on a grand scale and, it must be said, privately littered with the discarded hearts of young females. But Goethe does not gloss over the tensions at the core of the Faustian pact. Without the dubious *deus ex machina* at the end of the play, Faust would apparently have been abandoned to the black hag, Care, his basic attitude having delivered up only an ultimate emptiness. It is by no means clear that Goethe had really finished with his protagonist by the time of his own death. Part

II was nominally completed at the very end of the author's life, and published posthumously, but there is an abruptness and arbitrariness about the way the play is brought to a close that suggests that time had simply run out for Goethe.

The figure of Faust was subsequently absorbed wholesale into the European imagination, with little attention to Goethe's own apparent irresolution and ambivalence. Faust was seen as a prophet of progress, latterly of development. He consorted with the Devil, yes, but for honourable motives. His ambitions brought grief to others, but their grievous fates were the price of expanded horizons and enhanced human potential—in a word, of progress. Everything that stands in the way of progress must fall. Everything that can further it—such as nature, now rendered as natural resource—must be subordinated to it. Progress, latterly development, is a new normative standard that transcends conventional notions of morality and religion.

This is indeed what Goethe wrote. But it seems unlikely that he would be proud of the outcome of the Faustian experiment today, with the natural world in abject retreat before the armies of industry brandishing their triumphal ideology. Goethe himself was a devotee of nature and a passionate critic of the mechanistic, externalizing model of science. According to his own alternative model, living things are to be understood first and foremost in terms of their inner impulse to "increase their own existence," their conativity, the striving and aspiration which animate all beings. This striving, this deep-down impulse—the *ur-phenomenon*—is the ultimate and only source of the Good. It is surely for this reason that Goethe has Faust embody such striving. In unshackling Faust from antiquated moralities while giving his appetite for life free rein, Goethe was presumably intending to represent Faust as honouring nature at its source. To give expression to the thrust of nature in one's own being was presumably, in Goethe's view, to be truer than any overlay of reason or scriptural morality could be to the ultimate Good. The entire action of the play was, we might remember, a consequence of Faust's initial invocation of the Earth Spirit. It was to the

Earth Spirit that Faust turned for relief from his disaffection with a civilization based on reason, creed and convention: "all theory...is grey, but green is life's glad golden tree."[3]

In Goethe's science moreover, the outward forms of particular living things are explained not in terms of the cogs and wheels of constituent mechanisms but rather in terms of the influence of physical context. Every being is born into a particular set of physical conditions that, like the surrounding pieces of a jigsaw, determine the specific shape that its own striving for existence will take. Faust accordingly grasps that neither he nor others can increase their existence—fulfil their potential—unless the constraining material conditions of the feudal order are dismantled in favour of a new, more open—more modern—groundplan.

But the discordances at the end of the play suggest that already, even within the terms of the story, something was awry in Goethe's schema. The veritably epochal discordances that have accumulated in the actual roll-out of modernity suggest a catastrophic flaw in the founding narrative. Faust, the developer, has turned on Goethe, the devotee of nature, inaugurating an era of environmental holocaust. Mephistopheles, inadvertently invoked in the real world by Goethe's act of authorship just as he was inadvertently invoked in the play by a disaffected Faust, seems to be winning the day.

The details of Goethean science and philosophy have long since been forgotten, except by a handful of scholars, but the figure of Faust, complete with flaw, continues to inhabit, and exert directive force on, the Western imagination. In order to tackle the flaw it might be necessary to interrogate story with story. Story can have a taproot in mythical sources that will impart to it a logic, rigor and pattern-based form of insight, not to mention invocational efficacy, unavailable to mere analysis. Narrative logic may, in other words, yield insights and possibilities different from those available to reason, while story genuinely rooted in mythical sources may catalyze consequences unimaginable to reason.

[3] Johann Wolfgang Von Goethe, *Faust: Part Two*, trans. Philip Wayne (London: Penguin, 1959), 221.

Against this background of reflection then, let us re-launch the Faustian story, here, now, in the early 21st century. All that is required to do so are the right questions. If Faust reappeared in contemporary society—a society that has undergone two centuries of social and material development—how would the story play out? What would such a contemporary figure want? He would already possess everything the original Faust in his ascetic cloister lacked—affluence and total mobility; celebrity and worldly influence; religious choice; sexual freedom and the availability of women—though women, it must be noted, now also partake of that same freedom and enjoy those same opportunities. What, in these changed circumstances, could the devil offer him? The only thing a 21st century Faust would lack would be his soul. Would he miss it? Does soul even exist? What is it? If it does exist, it is of course the one thing Mephistopheles cannot bestow. Would Faust still need this thing called his soul? If so, from whom or what could he retrieve it? What, in a word, would Faust desire?

So let's take up the tale again. Professor Marcel Marianus is a highly successful academic in the American academy. The son of a German diplomat father and a Brazilian artist mother, he has "everything": the dark and sultry looks of his mother, the urbane intelligence and charm of his father, the finest mind that a protracted American/German postgraduate education can produce, academic prestige and even media celebrity. He is sought-after and influential. Although he is courted by his female students, and occasionally succumbs, he is smart enough to want his satisfactions to be of the highest order, so he values his marriage to a sophisticated and beautiful fellow academic, and tries not to jeopardize it. She is a professor of architecture with a high-powered career of her own. They share a polished and well-scripted intimacy, but this is an intimacy premised on mutual ambition. Neither would linger if the other were to cease serving their self-interest. We join Marcel as he is easing into a new position as a philosophy professor at a small but elite private university, Westin College.

Ardea
the tale

Marcel was riding in a cab late one night with the university president's stepson. As a recently appointed professor, Marcel had been elegantly wined and dined that evening at the president's residence—a relatively new suburban mansion, every room extravagantly lit up, like the properties in the real estate pages of newspapers. The boy, though listening to music through ear phones and messaging sporadically on his cell phone, was nevertheless stealing glances at his handsome companion, who gazed pensively out into the downtown night. Neither spoke to the other. It had been the boy's idea that they should prolong the evening by going to a club. He had proposed this as the family and several senior colleagues had stood at the front of the president's house, seeing Marcel off. The president had raised an eyebrow.

"This is the hour my son goes out," he explained, stroking the head of the family dog. "Every night. Just when the rest of us are going to bed." The boy had fastened his soft gaze on Marcel. Marcel was new to town.

"Why not!" Marcel had laughed. "Take me to the most decadent place you know, Guri." The president had made no objection.

Now however, in the back of the cab, Marcel was, in his pensive silence, uncomfortably reviewing the evening. The president, Mel Phillips, was, like Marcel, urbane and polished in manner, though ten or fifteen years older than his new appointee, and of a much more pronounced and alarming sensuality. Marcel, who was himself not above the odd dalliance, had sensed something far more sinister—something approaching real depravity—behind certain of the president's remarks, remarks that hinted at the availability of illicit pleasures. Why did he refer again and again in conversation to his "beautiful daughters," those dull-eyed girls in the background of the evening, simpering every time he looked their way? Whatever pleasures Mel had in mind, they were apparently offered as inducements, not to anything tangible, but, Marcel sensed, to mere allegiance. Mel had been courting him. This was understandable. Marcel had profile. With his mother's looks, his father's worldliness and the intellectual finesse his extravagant education had produced, Marcel was an academic heart throb, a veritable Indiana Jones amongst the frumpy denizens of the academy. Why wouldn't the president want the new professor on his side? But Marcel could not escape the feeling that more lay beneath the presidential flatteries than mere star-struck admiration. Though himself not innocent of conceit, nor even duplicity and ruthlessness where his own self-advancement was concerned, Marcel nevertheless possessed a certain moral complexity. His effortless enjoyment of both carnal pleasures and the privileges of success somehow did not wholly compromise the air of moral seriousness that hovered about him. Mel, on the other hand—Marcel could see at a glance—entirely lacked such complexity. To Mel, saddled with a coarser nature, how enviable Marcel's luminous blend of eros and gravitas must have seemed! And envy, Marcel sensed, had laid a snare. But what on earth could it be, he mused edgily. Well, whatever it was, he concluded, shaking off his disquiet and turning back to the boy, he would be ready.

Later, in a corner of a dark club, Marcel and Guri, seated

in black armchairs, faced each other across a small table, drinks in hand. The dance floor was throbbing, but the lounge area was somewhat removed from the noise. Marcel ran a hand through his shock of wavy black hair, parted in the middle, and asked Guri what he hoped to do with his life when his studies were complete. Guri was uncertain. He ventured however that the life of a philosophy professor seemed not unappealing, if the rumours he had heard about Marcel on campus were true.

"What rumours are those," Marcel queried.

"Oh," Guri said, "rumours that you have an apartment in Paris and a visiting position at the Sorbonne, that your friends are film stars and that you have been known to travel in a private jet."

Marcel shrugged casually and nodded.

"There are also rumours," Guri continued, a little more hesitantly, "that you keep a 'red phone,' a mobile number exclusively for the use of your female students."

Marcel raised his eyebrows. "Female *ex*-students, *please*, Guri," he exclaimed.

Guri added, laughing a little truculently, that he was sure the life of a philosopher could hardly be so glamorous. Marcel laughed in turn, and suggested they put the rumours to the test. He looked around the smoky nightclub and said he'd wager he could kiss any girl in the room before the night was out.

"You choose the girl," he offered.

"And if you win?" Guri asked.

Marcel looked at him levelly as he sipped his drink. "We can decide on my reward later tonight," he replied. "Now," he insisted, indicating the dance floor with a quick movement of his chin, "choose."

Guri smiled, pleased, and pointed to a particularly buxom young woman in a slithery dress. Marcel rose from his chair, and, as he left to begin his mission, he deftly and surreptitiously squeezed Guri's hand.

After Marcel disappeared into the crush, Guri checked his email, went to the bar, bought a cocktail, drifted out onto a balcony to smoke, spoke into his phone, and returned to the bar. Even while he talked his eyes roamed the crowd; there was no sign of Marcel under the dance lights. Guri resumed his seat in the lounge where some drunken friends from college found him, gathered around him rowdily for a few minutes, then lurched on. Guri sank back into his chair, replaced his ear-phones, and popped a couple of pills from a gold-plated pill-box he took from his pocket. Finally, after forty-five minutes, Marcel came into view, steering the designated girl onto the dance floor. Guri watched as Marcel drew the girl to him and started to stroke her neck softly. As she tilted her head back he momentarily buried his face in her breast then proceeded to caress her neck with countless soft, expert kisses. The girl yielded her whole skimpily satin-clad body to his close embrace, but Marcel was not so absorbed that he could not look up and, for a moment, gazing over the girl's bare shoulder, meet Guri's eyes.

During the following week, Guri, who was already majoring in philosophy, signed up for another philosophy class, the one, of course, taught by Marcel. Although Marcel was new to the university, three weeks into the semester attendance in his class was high. There were forty or so students in the room. Guri was a little late, and slipped into the back row. Marcel was discoursing on Plato. Totally absorbed in his own rather mannered performance, he did not notice Guri's entrance. *The Good Life* was his topic. What constitutes a good life, he was asking the students, looking up at them and furrowing his handsome brow appealingly. Is the good life one devoted merely to pleasures? A male student in the front row ventured that one would have to distinguish between higher and lower pleasures before answering the question. Other students offered examples of higher and lower pleasures—the pleasures of the senses, for lower, and the pleasures of reading, friendship, even good works, for higher.

"Ah," said Marcel, "so being *good*, in the sense of according a moral structure to one's life, may produce pleasure! Is this what Plato meant when he declared that *the just man is happy*? Is according a moral structure to one's life the ultimate source of happiness?"

Around the room there were pious if uncertain nods. The rewards of being "just" did indeed seem, to most of the students, to trump the rewards of mere pleasure seeking.

"But," Marcel persisted, "do the seeming rewards of being just really accrue, in the final analysis, from being *perceived* to be just? What if you could have all the benefits of being *perceived* to be just without really *being* just—if you could consistently put your own interests before the interests of others yet still be seen by them as having impeccable integrity?"

Expanding on this question, Marcel put it in Plato's terms: *is it better actually to be just or merely to have the reputation for justice?*

"Suppose," he went on, "you had to choose between two options. The first option allowed you to follow your own desires in all your dealings with people, yet, because of wealth, fame or celebrity, you could get away with everything, so that even those you had wronged dared not speak against you because they knew that others would reproach and spurn them for doing so. This might be like having Plato's mythical 'ring of Gyges,' which conferred invisibility, so the wearer could do whatever they wished, even to the point of satisfying lusts, with total anonymity and impunity, all the while maintaining an outer appearance of perfect probity. The second option was the complete reverse. It required you to be considerate, honest and unselfish in all your dealings, putting others first, even if this placed you at such a disadvantage that not only were your good deeds and character not recognized but you were vilified for misdeeds and vices of which you were totally innocent."

"In other words," Marcel wound up, "is it worth being good if no-one will ever find out that you are? And is it okay to be bad if you can at the same time make people believe you are good? If you can live life to the full, winning wealth, power, prestige and popularity, by being bad, while only disadvantaging yourself and losing influence by being good, is there any reason to be good? What is at stake in this choice?"

There was silence in the room. Finally a conservative-looking woman, older than the other students, intoned with a slightly Australian accent,

"What shall it profit a man if he gain the whole world but lose his own soul?"

Marcel gave her a studied look.

"Indeed," he said. "And what *shall* it profit a man? If I know that at my funeral there will be hundreds of people not only speaking well of me but thinking well of me, because my wealth and influence have, one way or another, rubbed off on them and benefitted them, even though it was gained at deep injury and cost to individuals now too disempowered to speak against me, *will* the loss of my 'soul' matter to me? Would I really trade all that wealth and reputation for the possession of 'soul' if maintaining soul meant a lonely and disgraced funeral, the defection of my family to those who had injured me, and obliteration by history?"

The silence deepened in the room. The woman with the Australian accent spoke softly.

"To lose one's soul," she pointed out, "might be to lose one's immortality. Didn't Plato believe in the immortality of the soul?"

"Yes," Marcel conceded. "But when he asserted that the just man is happy, he wasn't arguing that one should be just in order to gain eternal life; he was arguing that the just life is its own reward. Only the person who makes morality his goal will attain true happiness. And what I am asking is whether that claim is true. Is it what we *are* that gives us a sense of self-worth and hence of satisfaction, or what others *think* we are? And can we ultimately even distinguish between these two conditions ourselves?"

The woman, at whom the other students were now looking expectantly, persevered.

"Maybe the sense in which the authentic person is happy

is tied up with the idea of immortality," she hazarded. "If the Good is, as Plato also held, at the core of existence, then bringing one's life into alignment with it might mean that one becomes…uh, um,…or rather partakes of, the eternal essence of things."

She flushed. Marcel was staring at her.

"Hmm," he responded after a pause, "nice argument, er, what is your name?"

"June," the student replied.

"Nice argument, June. But *is* 'the Good' at the core of existence? Is the universe governed by moral law, or only by physical laws? Hasn't science shown us that the universe is morally neutral—that things happen exclusively as a result of the laws of physics, rather than in accordance with any moral law? And in that case, why should a person be good if it would profit them, in this, their only actual life, to be bad? Why should wrong-doing—assuming one could get away with it—make one unhappy?"

Guri was excited at June's suggestion that goodness was somehow key to an eternal order of things. He sensed a nourishing potential in this idea and was disappointed at Marcel's refusal to follow it up. But wasn't it true that science had indeed, as Marcel said, shown that moral law was in no way inherent in the nature of reality? In which case, what was there to follow up…?

When it was time to bring the class to an end, Marcel held up a pre-publication copy of his new book, *Modernity and Melancholia*, and indicated that the themes he had touched upon in the lecture were explored there in greater depth. He nodded perfunctorily to Guri as he left the room. Outside, Guri overheard a clump of female students giggling over the new professor's reputation for scandal. They speculated about his off-campus movements and haunts and wondered where one might go to "bump into" him. Clearly the questions he had raised had barely registered with them. In Guri's case the questions had indeed registered. He left the classroom feeling dejected, but pondering with even greater urgency where he too might next "bump into" his dark-eyed professor.

At home that afternoon in his luxurious and spacious, industrial-chic apartment, Marcel was arranging books on the shelves in his study. His wife was away at a conference. Talking apologetically into his red phone he took down a thick, leather-bound art folio and opened it on the desk. The folio held exquisite miniature paintings and engravings of erotica, both oriental and occidental. He leafed through them, inspecting them closely while he talked, explaining to the person on the other end of the phone why he had not been able to show up for a drink, assuring her that he wanted very much to see her again. When the conversation was over he put the folio back in a row of folders, and took down another. This one contained oriental miniatures of birds—ducks and geese, but especially herons and cranes. Again, he leafed through the collection long and lingeringly, with a hint of melancholy and a glint of obsession, before returning the folio to its place, and, in a gesture of possessiveness, running a fine white finger across the spines of the many volumes of erotic and oriental art that occupied the same shelf.

Marcel's wife, Mirielle, arrived home early that evening. An extremely elegant woman in her late-thirties, in high heels and with plumped-up lips, she pressed her body to Marcel's in greeting. After a five minute chat however, she disappeared into her office, from whence he could hear her in an earnest phone discussion with a colleague. Already a full professor, she had very significant teaching and administrative responsibilities in the school of architecture, responsibilities she carried willingly, with relish and aplomb. When she reemerged from the office, Marcel invited her to join him for a drink, but she remarked—rather casually in the circumstances, Marcel thought—that two of her new colleagues would shortly be arriving for dinner. She had booked a caterer to deliver a seafood spread, but was busy now preparing the table.

"Perhaps you could have mentioned it to me," Marcel remarked evenly.

"Darling," she said, coming to him, "I'm so sorry. I only invited them today, and there was not the tiniest *chink* in the schedule to call you. You don't mind too much, do you? Wilber and Darian are very close to the president, and I thought you'd like to meet them. They are negotiating a development deal with Wilkins. You know Wilkins is the biggest architectural firm in this state? They've won a swathe of international awards for their integrated cities in China. Mel is in on this deal, though I'm not sure in what way. The development is up the coast. It's really a tower-city, a circle of high-rises linked by covered aerial roadways and built around a marina. There will be a covered entrance to the marina on the ocean side—a huge casino." Here Mirielle did a quick sketch showing a sun face with a wide mouth, like the old luna parks, though in minimalist style.

"The boats," she continued, pointing to the sketch, "will pass through the casino on their way in and out of the marina. The city will face the sea and its main gateway will be the casino. I thought if I invited Darian and Wilber over I might find out a bit more about the plans, and show them some of my own work in integrated hydrological design. I don't think they realize the potential for running the entire city on tidal power, together with solar and wind from the top of the towers. Each tower could also rest on a desalination plant. The whole complex could supply itself with energy and water. It'd be the first city of its kind in this country…Besides," Mirielle added, twisting one of Marcel's curls around a finger, "both these guys are as keen as mustard to meet you! Mel has obviously been talking about you."

Planting a kiss below his ear as expert as the kisses Marcel had administered to the girl in the club, Mirielle again left the room, to change from her tailored suit into evening wear, leaving Marcel to drink alone.

Meanwhile Guri was attending other classes. His favorite philosophy professor, after Marcel, was Ardea, who lectured in environmental ethics. If he mentioned Ardea Dunne at home, his step-father's lip curled. That *that* fool of a woman had ever wormed her way into Westin College, he would snap, was beyond belief. This endeared Ardea to Guri, arousing a sense of allegiance in him. Ardea's class was not particularly well attended. Although she was youngish and slender and moved gracefully, she wore glasses and no make-up and dressed in a rather counter-cultural style that failed to impress wealthy students. Those students who did attend, apart from Guri and one or two others, including June, also inclined towards the counter-cultural in appearance, with tousled hair and colourful, mismatching outfits.

Whereas Guri never spoke in Marcel's class, in Ardea's he was voluble. He found, to his own surprise, that he was on the side of the endangered species, the ferns and sedges, the high plains and dune fields, the honey bees, tree frogs and humpback whales, all collapsing and vanishing under the assault of an empire of industry that now knew no bounds at all, that was moving in for the final, terrible capture or kill of *everything*, everything that moved and breathed with a life that was not human. Each week Ardea prefaced her lecture with some instance of eco-catastrophe or ecocide occurring *at that moment* somewhere on the planet. One week it might be an oil spill on a coral reef; another week a climate-change-induced wildfire in a million hectares of national park; another week again a new disease that had suddenly erupted in a species of wildlife that was in consequence, in a matter of a few short years, slipping towards extinction. More than a quarter of all mammal and bird species on earth today, together with one in eight reptile species and one in three amphibians are now endangered, she told them. In one class she read out a passage describing the impressions of some of the earliest Europeans to explore America.

"In 1524," she read, "Verrazano reported smelling cedars a hundred leagues from land. Other [explorers] told of sailing through vast beds of floating flowers. Ducks, turkey, deer, lynx greeted them in unimaginable abundance. Whales so crowded the waters that they were navigational hazards. Cape Cod was named for its cod-clotted waters. Salmon ran thick in every Atlantic river from Labrador to the Hudson. Lobsters were so common that they were used throughout New England for potato fertilizer, pig food, fish bait…all gone, now. Islands once packed shore to shore with walrus or seals or nesting seabirds are now empty…."[1] Before she could finish reading out the passage, that went on to list several of the atrocities committed against particular species in the process of European colonization, she choked up, to the intense discomfort of the class.

"*Why*," she asked the helpless little group? "*Why* is our civilization allowing—presiding over—the sheer destruction of the planet? It's scarcely even conceivable, yet it is what is happening. How is it possible?" Clearly, Ardea was herself at a total loss for an answer.

"It's the money," volunteered one student. "People are exploiting nature for the money."

"But there's money to be made from slavery," rejoined Ardea. "That doesn't mean that slavery is tolerated."

Guri spoke up. "Slaves are human, and in our society humans have rights, but plants and animals don't have rights. So while it's not okay to destroy people in order to profit other people, it is considered okay to destroy plants and animals for human benefit."

Warmly affirming Guri's contribution, Ardea nevertheless pushed on. "But *why*," she asked, "*why* does our society accord rights to *human* beings but not to *non*-human beings?"

"Well, humans are special," Guri obliged. "We are different from other animals."

"In what way?" inquired Ardea.

"We're more intelligent," Guri pointed out.

"Why should intelligence matter, Guri? Should people

who are very smart have a greater right to life than people who are less smart?"

The whole class agreed that that would be a bad idea!

"Why should we rank excellences in the first place," Ardea demanded. "Humans have a form of intelligence appropriate to humans, while dogs, fish and microbes each have forms of intelligence appropriate to their own kind. What use would human reason be to fish, and what use would fish intelligence be to us? Each species has precisely the excellences required for its own needs. Birds can navigate and fly. Fish can breathe in water. Do we rank them above humans, morally speaking, because these are excellences that humans lack?"

Another student entered the debate.

"Isn't the fact that humans now dominate the planet evidence of our superiority," he asked.

"Well," Ardea countered, "if a pathogen wiped out the human race and colonized all other species as its hosts, would that be evidence of the superiority of the pathogen?"

"But pathogens are primitive," another student interjected; "we are more important than microbes because we are much more complex—much more sophisticated beings."

"Why is it more valuable to be complex," Ardea quizzed. "Isn't complexity only of value if it increases adaptiveness? And the oldest extant species on the planet—those species which have proved best adapted—are amongst the simplest. For example, the Horseshoe Shrimp, a tiny little fresh-water crustacean, appeared on earth two hundred million years ago and remains virtually unchanged today. Two hundred million years is quite a long time when you consider that the entire era of the dinosaurs, from beginning to end, lasted less than that. In any case, the Horseshoe Shrimp never evolved into anything more complex because it was already perfect for its niche. In that sense complexity is evidence of *im*perfection," Ardea concluded, laughing, with a triumphant little flourish.

June, who had been silent to this point, now spoke up.

"Some people think humans are special because we are

made in the image of God," she ventured. "We have souls, which other animals are thought to lack."

Ardea, used to arguing in secular terms and discomforted by the terms of religion, was a little taken aback.

"What do you mean by 'soul', June?"

"Well," June responded, "I mean the immortal part of our existence. Not necessarily the personality, but the part that endures for eternity."

Raising her eyebrows, Ardea replied, "What part is that? How do we know we possess such a part?"

In a soft but firm voice, June stated, "Through revelation. Through the covenant that God has established with humanity in the course of history. The covenant sets out the Law by which we may live as people of God. If we follow the Law, we rise above mere matter and enter into a relationship with God. And through that relationship, we partake of eternity...."

"Goodness," Ardea exclaimed, "that's an interesting line of thought, June. It rests on faith though, which not everyone shares. Philosophical arguments rest on reason. Everyone can, at least in principle, accept the dictates of reason. And from the viewpoint of reason, to appeal to revelation in order to establish a notion of soul does not prove the case for human exceptionalism—by which I mean the view that sees humanity as somehow set apart from and above the rest of nature."

June frowned slightly. "I know that, Ardea. But perhaps there is more to environmental ethics than can be established by reason."

Guri, who had been following the exchange intently, nodded excitedly. Ardea assented.

"You're probably right, June. I need to think about it. Let's take this topic up again next week."

After class, Guri approached Ardea familiarly and asked if he could join her for coffee. She agreed warmly; this had become routine with them. She seemed unaware that he was the president's son; in any case, he knew that even had she been aware, it would have made no difference. She would have met him on equal terms. She was untenured, peripheral to politicking in the philosophy department and the administration; she cared nothing for the small badges of rank so coveted by her colleagues, and consequently she lacked influence; she was even, as far as Guri knew, single, an unclaimed woman. Yet none of this seemed to matter to her. She had taken Guri into her fold, and Guri found, to his surprise, it *was* a fold, a refuge, a place in which he felt relaxed and safe. This strange new feeling was, he realized, a result of the fact that he trusted her. He started looking forward enthusiastically to her classes.

The following week however Ardea opened the hour with a particularly harrowing instance of ecological atrocity. As soon as the students were settled in their seats and the classroom screen had been unfurled, she projected a large image of an elephant collapsed on its knees. Its entire face had been hacked off, almost to its ears.

"This is Satao," she began, but there were already tears spilling down her cheeks.

"Please bear to look at him. He was until last week the largest elephant still alive in Kenya, a 'tusker,' meaning that his tusks were so long they reached almost to the ground. He roamed the Tsavo National Park for 50 years and was well known throughout the country. But last week he was killed by a poacher's poisoned arrow. Whether the killers cut off his face before or after he died is not known...." Ardea paused to let the students take in the graphic image. Several of them were also now in tears.

"Because the image is so shocking," she resumed, "I'd like us just to sit with it today, rather than going ahead with the scheduled lecture. Of course the killing of Satao is not an isolated incident. According to *National Geographic*, 100,000 elephants have been killed by poachers in just the last 3 years. In 2011 alone, one in every twelve elephants in Africa was slaughtered. The elephant population on the continent is crashing. And all these deaths are as brutal as Satao's, causing untold suffering not only for the victims but for members of elephant families left behind and for youngsters orphaned...."

But Satao's death is different inasmuch as it comes with a *story*. He was an iconic personality, nationally cherished, a celebrity really, his life well documented. His intelligence was legendary: aware of the poachers' intent—he had, after all, witnessed the fate of so many of his comrades at poachers' hands—he would hide his tusks by standing amongst bushes whenever humans were around. And normally he kept to safer precincts. But recently there had been big rains, and a flush of growth in the eastern, less patrolled areas of the park. Lots of other elephants were heading over towards these lush new pastures. Satao waited and waited, but eventually, against his better judgment, he joined them...and this was the outcome." Ardea wiped away more tears as she gestured towards the image...."In any case, because Satao happened to be just a bit larger than his relatives, his death, as I've said, is not merely a statistic but is being told as story. And story can carry moral meaning in a way that mere statistics can't.... June, I've been thinking about what you said last week. About revelation. About the Law. I'm not a Christian or a Jew. Or a Muslim. But still I think what you said about environmental ethics was important. Perhaps there is something more to it than can be established by reason. Or rather, there's more to it than can be *conveyed* by reason. The kind of moral meaning that compels can perhaps only be conveyed by stories. Which is why religions are tied to founding narratives. I must say my own strongest impulse, in confronting this image of Satao, is somehow to tie it to such stories, to add his picture, his story, to the sacred galleries of martyrs, prophets, saints ...to the scenes of sacrifice, of crucifixion, through which 'the Law' is renewed between 'God' and human beings...."

June, who was also dabbing her cheeks, accepted Ardea's overture.

"Yes," she murmured, "one doesn't have to be a Christian, Jew or Muslim to believe in Law. Indigenous peoples also live by the Law. In Australia, where I come from, Aboriginal people call it Dreaming Law. And yes, it is communicated via stories....One difference though, between the stories that convey Dreaming Law and those that convey Law in the

Abrahamic faiths is that the stories of the Abrahamic tradition were written down and so at a certain point became fixed in time. Today we can reinterpret these stories in contemporary terms but we can't really add new ones. New Dreaming stories, on the other hand, are still being discovered by Aboriginal people all the time, as historical and environmental circumstances change...."

Other students were anxious to join the discussion.

"What is 'the Law' in the Abrahamic faiths, June?" a boy wearing a vintage hip hop tee-shirt asked.

"Well, Jake," June replied, "the Law was established via a Covenant between the Israelites and God. In the pre-literate era, the Covenant did evolve through time. The first version was revealed to Noah after the Flood, when God promised never to destroy the world again. The rainbow was God's signature to this first agreement." June smiled shyly and added, as an aside, "We could call this the Climate Change Covenant, Ardea. Then there was a succession of messengers or prophets, each one updating and elaborating the Covenant in response to changing historical circumstances. Abraham, for example, was instructed by God to add circumcision to the agreement. Then there was Moses, of course. He brought the Ten Commandments down from Mount Sinai, straight from the hand of God, but 'Mosaic Law' includes lots of other rules about how to organize society and these are scattered through the early books of the Old Testament. Jesus stripped these very detailed rules down to the Sermon on the Mount. According to this 'new covenant,' God forgives our sins, rather than insisting, as Mosaic Law did, that the 'wages of sin are death.' And the new covenant is offered to all peoples, not only to Jews. For Christians, Christ was the final prophet, but for Muslims of course it was Mohammed who received the final revelation, which was spelt out by him in the Qur'an as Sharia Law—also a very detailed set of rules.

"But," Jake persisted, "what *is* the agreement, what's the core? What are people signing up to? What are the 'sins' for which we'll be punished or forgiven?"

"Well," said June, glancing a little nervously at Ardea, "I

guess the core of the agreement is that people should become one with God, they should acknowledge Him and worship Him as their one true God. That's what God wants from us. The core sin is to stray from God, not to believe in the prophets."

"Oh," Ardea groaned audibly. "'The Lord thy God is a jealous God.' Isn't that just a blueprint for intolerance, for endless war and persecution?! Why on earth should it matter to God whether or not people worship Him? Surely He didn't create humans just so He could have followers, like friends on Facebook!"

June looked apologetic. "Mmm," she admitted, "it doesn't sound very good, the way I put it, I admit. But I think the idea is more that, through the Covenant, the people become God's and, more importantly, God becomes the people's. God is giving Himself to the people. Since He is so much mightier than they, this is a supreme act of grace. But God knows that people will only grasp its significance if they in turn are delivered over wholly to Him. He asks them to give themselves wholly to Him so that they can grasp his gift of Himself to them. It is this giving of Himself that is the true purpose of the Covenant. But the tangible gift that emanates from the Covenant is, I think, the Law. God's gift of Himself is the gift of teaching people how to live. When people live right, when they live by the Law, they become knitted back into something, a greater unity, which is indeed transcendent."

"Hmm, I think I see what you mean," murmured Ardea. "And, as you mentioned earlier, the idea of Law can be found in other religions too, religions that aren't monotheistic. As I recall, it appears as Dharma in both Buddhism and Hinduism, and as Dao in Daoism. The words 'dharma' and 'dao' both mean 'way.' And Dharma is a Way of kindness and reverence for all life while Dao is likewise a Way of harmony with all things."

June nodded.

"And Dreaming Law," she continued, "is a Way par excellence—it tells people how to nourish and sustain 'country', meaning, umm, living land, the living cosmos of Aboriginal people. By looking after country, in accordance with Dreaming Law, one is also looking after people, and in meshing people and country together and looking after them one becomes part of something far greater, an order of eternal regeneration, of eternal Life. So, all in all, it's clear that this notion of a moral Law, of a Law of Life at the heart of Creation, is common to many religions. Actually, 'sharia' means 'way' too, 'the clear, well-trodden path to water.' Not that I can speak for Islam," June added hurriedly. "I'm a Christian, so can really only speak for Christianity, and only from my own particular perspective. My husband is a Methodist minister, so we are always discussing these questions. And both of us do try to understand the Abrahamic tradition in wider terms. I guess I'd say that, by asking us to enter into a covenant with God, the Abrahamic faiths are just seeking to convey that there is a unitive aspect to Creation, and hence a moral purpose to the universe. This purpose is universal—it is the same for all people. There is not one Law for people who worship, say, Astarte, and another for people who worship Osiris or Zeus or Shiva. There really is a right way to live for human beings—for *any* intelligent beings! The Law is just the articulation of this right way. And the fact that such a right way of living exists—the fact that it is actually part of the fabric of reality, there for us to discover—implies that the universe is not just a blind play of chance and necessity, but something greater or higher, something with purpose, to which we can belong or in which we can consciously participate. I think that the universe under this moral, purposeful aspect is what I mean when I talk about God," June added thoughtfully. Then she smiled. "As an old Aboriginal friend of mine used to say, the universe isn't an empty shed. There's something in it!…Of course, to what extent we can discover the Law at any given historical moment will depend on all kinds of circumstances—which is why prophets or buddhas or inspired teachers, or, in Aboriginal societies, storymen and women, are needed. But that's just a way of saying that we receive Law via revelation…."

The entire class was by now gazing at June in awe.

"So do you think it would be consistent with Christianity, June, to see Satao as a new prophet," Ardea asked, "and his life as a new revelation of the Law?"

"Well," June hesitated, "I'm not sure whether Christians would agree to this, because for them Christ's word was the final word, the final covenant. That's what defines them as Christians. But I suppose there's no reason why one shouldn't tie new narratives, such as the story of Satao, to the narratives of the Abrahamic tradition, only then I don't think we could still call the resulting religion, 'Christianity,' even though it shared founding narratives with Christianity."

Guri was visibly excited, almost bouncing in his seat.

"But isn't that just it, June," he burst out. "Isn't our problem precisely that we stop each religion in its tracks and slap a prophet's name on it, instead of being open to ongoing revelations—as the early Hebrews were? If we just saw all religions as strands of a single nameless but always unfolding thing…Religion with a capital R…wouldn't we be better off? I mean, the Abrahamic stories could be, kind of, a framework for revelation for some peoples at a certain stage of history, and the Hindu stories could be a framework for other peoples, but everyone could remain open to new revelations of the Law, new messengers…such as Satao! Everyone could tie the new stories back to their own original stories in ways that made sense for their tradition…."

"Well, yes," June agreed, still a little uncertain about the ground she was treading, "Satao's life would indeed work well as a revelation in the Abrahamic tradition because in that tradition the covenant was always cut in blood."

"Wow!" exclaimed Guri, glowing-eyed. "The covenant was cut in blood!"

"What do you mean, June?" asked Ardea, her eyes also widening.

"Well, in ancient days in the Middle East—and actually in many parts of the world—before legal documents had been invented, covenants or contracts were established between people by means of a fairly elaborate ritual. This involved sacrificing an animal and cutting it in two. They would lay the two halves out and each party to the covenant would then pass between them, as if to say, 'If I break this agreement may God do to me as we have done to this animal!' This was called 'cutting the covenant.' Later in the ceremony, each party would cut the palm of their hand then rub their palm to the palm of the other party to mingle their blood. This was to show that the two of them were now one. Each party was also required to carve a separate wound in their flesh so that the scar would later bear testimony to the covenant. The blood covenant was no light matter! Two people who had been through it together were bound indissolubly—everything they owned now belonged to the other. They were obliged to defend and look after each other unto death. To break the blood covenant was unthinkable. Anyone who broke it would not only be killed but totally erased from the memory of the community....The blood covenant was the prototype for the covenant between God and humanity. In all the biblical stories of the Old and New Testaments there are references to this ceremony: when God gave the Law to Abraham, for example, Abraham was required to circumcise himself and impose the practice of circumcision on all the Israelites, so that the scar of circumcision would serve as a mark of the Covenant between God and his people. And the ultimate example of God renewing the blood covenant was that of the crucifixion: Christ was sacrificed, his blood spilled, so that a New Covenant between God and humanity could be established."

Ardea, like the rest of the class, was enthralled by the idea of the blood covenant. "Do you think we could see the great shedding of animal blood that is now occurring across the planet as a sign, a call, to a new covenant?" she asked June. "Could we indeed invest Satao with this office? Could we take his life as a revelation, a cry for a return to a Law that embraces all of Creation?"

June sighed. "I'm not sure Christians would like this, Ardea. They do insist that Christ was the last prophet. As I said, that's what defines us as Christians. And besides, they might be offended by the idea of God choosing an animal as his messenger."

"Why should they be!" Guri erupted.

From the other side of the room, another student, a young girl in a velvet outfit topped with a trilby hat, joined in.

"Yes, why should they be! I've read that elephants have brains six times larger than ours! They can communicate across large distances—hundreds of miles. They have gifts of knowing that we can't even comprehend, that we don't begin to understand! They're matriarchal too and they care for one another far better than we in our human communities do. They'd make much better prophets than us!"

"But what about a chicken," asked a girl who hadn't spoken up yet. "Could a chicken count as a prophet?"

"Or a cockroach," smirked Jake. "Could a cockroach count?"

The girl in the trilby responded heatedly. "To ask that just shows how wrong it is to group all nonhuman beings together under one category: 'animals', as if they are all the same! Why don't we just call them 'beings'? Then there would be beings who were capable of becoming prophets and beings who weren't. No problem!"

"Anyway," Guri interrupted, "what does it matter if Christians don't accept animals as prophets? Maybe it's time for people who don't belong to the old text-based religions to take the lead! To embrace the Religion with No Name, the Religion of Unfolding Revelation. And Satao can be our first prophet!"

A Chinese exchange student who rarely spoke in class chuckled.

"The Religion with No Name sounds a lot like Daoism," he said. "*The Dao that can be told is not the eternal Dao. The name that can be named is not the eternal name*'."

Ardea laughed too, switching her computer off so that the image of Satao would not be blasphemed.

"Besides," the Chinese student continued, "the name, 'Satao,' is a perfect fit with Daoism." He walked over to the white board and wrote up, "Sa Tao" and next to it a string of Chinese characters. "If we use the old Wade Giles transcription," he explained, "instead of pinyin, 'Dao' is written as 'Tao.' 'Sa Tao' can then mean, 'Melancholy Way' or even 'Way of the Sound of the Wind,' which might suggest the loss or emptiness that results when we lose the true Way."

"Ah yes," said Ardea. "Satao as a revelation of the desecration of the Way."

A Chinese girl sitting next to the student who had just spoken chimed in crisply. "Satao would make a very good prophet or martyr for Chinese people today, since it's from China that the demand for ivory is coming. People want ivory to make stupid trinkets. They care nothing for the great beings who are slaughtered to provide them. I'd like to see statues of Satao, slain, just as he appears in the picture you have shown, Ardea, in Daoist temples in China today."

"And what about Ganesha," the girl in the trilby hat added. "There are statues of Ganesha everywhere in India. Why not place statues of Satao next to them, to show people how Dharma is being violated today! That'd be a way of tying Satao's story to the founding narratives of Hinduism…."

The hour was drawing to a close but no-one, least of all Ardea, wanted to end the discussion. However, the room was booked so they could not linger overtime. Ardea signalled they would have to stop, but Jake, the boy in the hip hop tee-shirt, was anxious to speak.

"Suppose we start this Religion with No Name," he said to Guri. "Who decides who the new prophets are? Who decides which revelations really do reveal the Law and which ones are fake?"

"Uh," replied Guri, "I guess the people do, Jake, just as they always have. I guess a real revelation is one which, in their hearts, people recognize to be true, even if they've been denying this truth, or avoiding it, till then. The prophet is just the one who articulates it in a way they can't ignore any more…like 'an inconvenient truth,'" Guri grinned. Everyone rolled their eyes….

"Okay," Jake persisted, "but if this is how the Religion with No Name works, how will it prevent war? Won't the followers of Satao soon become just as intolerant of the followers of, say, Christ or Buddha as the followers of traditional religions have always been of one another?"

Guri shook his head. "No, I don't think so. Everyone following the Religion with No Name would know that the prophet is not the religion, the prophet's word is not the Law, that revelation is never-ending, that it can't be pinned down, that it is always being renewed. For the Religion with No Name there can be no such thing as dogma...."

"Yes!" June piped up again. "That's how it is in Aboriginal societies. New stories are added to the existing lore of Dreaming stories by negotiation amongst the people themselves. If an extraordinary event occurs, or someone has a big, significant dream, the community considers it—they kind of meditate on it for a while—and then it is quietly either taken up as a genuine revelation or let go. The new story has to be consistent with Dreaming Law, but it might add new insights, insights that the community needs at that point."

Students waiting for the next class were lining up outside the door.

Ardea signalled again, but added, "There's just one more thing I'd like to say before thanking you all, and especially June, for such an inspiring tribute to Satao. Some of you might now be wondering whether environmental ethics is indeed a form of religion. Opponents of environmentalism often accuse 'greenies' of this, implying that environmentalism is a kind of self-indulgent mysticism rather than an outlook based on reason. I want to emphasize that environmental ethics can be defended in terms of reason alone, just as human ethics can. Just as we can care for people out of compassion and a rational appreciation of their entitlement to consideration, without any kind of appeal to religion, so we can care for all creatures in the same way. However, environmental ethics is also a reminder of a Way that was once, as we've seen, central to many traditions which interpreted reality in moral and perhaps transcendent as well as material terms. In some of the oldest religious traditions, humans were called to care not only for people but for all of Creation.

This was the Way. In this sense, environmental ethics can serve as a bridge to such an ancient, indeed mystical view of Creation. But whether we regard morality as based on reason or religion, the point remains that perhaps only through stories will it acquire emotional force. Perhaps only through stories will we ultimately connect emotionally with the rest of life. So," Ardea concluded, half-smiling, "please feel free to bring to class any other images or stories that have struck you with the force of revelation, calling humanity to renew its covenant with Creation. Perhaps we can create a gallery of nonhuman prophets and martyrs right here in our classroom for Guri's Religion with No Name."

As the class dispersed, Ardea felt pleased but also slightly rueful to see Guri walking away deep in conversation with June, his regular coffee date with herself forgotten.

Though at ease with Ardea, Guri remained fretful where his other favourite philosophy professor was concerned. His infatuation with Marcel increased. Taking every opportunity to encounter him, he attended his classes, sought to ambush him on his way to lunch in the staff club, even pestered him from time to time on his red phone. Marcel was affectionate, calling him his lion cub, but nevertheless refrained from repeating the seduction of the first night. Occasionally he would however take Guri out for a pre-dinner drink. On one such occasion, Guri mentioned his friendship with Ardea. To his dismay, Marcel almost sneered.

"What would you want with a non-entity like her," he asked. This was a side of the normally suave Marcel that Guri had not previously seen. Confounded, the boy nevertheless rallied to Ardea's defence.

"Ardea is...she is...*genuine*," he blurted out, without aforethought.

"*Genuine*," scoffed Marcel, instantly piqued. "What does *that* mean, for God's sake?"

"It means she stands up for what she thinks is important and doesn't give, um, a toss whether other people agree with her. She really *cares*," Guri added, a little desperately.

"We all care," snapped Marcel. "About different things. I care about philosophy. You care about…well, I don't know, music. Your father cares about the university. What does caring prove?"

"I don't mean it like that," Guri stammered. "She cares about something that can't repay her. The earth. She cares about it not because it will boost her career…or entertain her …or make her look good…or even thank her. She *really* cares."

Marcel turned aside in disgust.

"Well, if caring turns you into a frump like her," he remarked meanly, "I can't see the point of it."

Too shocked to reply, Guri reached inside his jacket for his pill box.

Later that afternoon Marcel arrived home to a message from his wife on their landline. She would not be home for dinner as she had a last minute appointment with Darian to discuss the Wilkins development. Marcel was to order dinner from a delivery service. Slightly ruffled, but unwilling to admit it to himself, he put together a plate of smoked salmon and antipasto from the fridge and, with a bottle of wine, retired to his study. Mid-evening, he heard Mirielle return and go straight to the bathroom. He emerged from his study with the half-empty bottle in hand and settled himself on the sofa in the living area to await Mirielle, pouring two glasses of wine in the meantime. In a few moments Mirielle joined him. She was wearing a tight, low-cut black dress. Marcel wondered how she had managed to change into it before going out to dinner. Perhaps she had been back to the apartment in the course of the afternoon? She had an unaccustomed flush, and seemed slightly tousled, her eyes very bright. She came straight over and nestled up to him on the sofa, letting the black straps slip from her shoulders. Automatically he started to undress her as she leaned across him, launching into an account, with less than her usual composure, of the night's events. Wilber and Darian wanted her in on the deal, it seemed, and the deal was big, beyond her wildest dreams. There was Chinese money behind it. It was not merely a Wilkins development but a Wilkins Heng-Hu development and the web of investment interests led all the way up to Congress. Planning would not be a problem because a number of politicians were on board. It was a multi-billion dollar proposal, and Darian had said they wanted her on the architectural team, specifically on the hydrology side.

"I think this is it, Marcel," she whispered as he absentmindedly kissed her hair, "the break I've been waiting for. Out of academia. Into the big time."

She laid her head back against Marcel's shoulder and closed her eyes. He responded by doing the only thing he could—gathering his wife up in his arms and carrying her to the bedroom.

The next morning Marcel received a message from the president. He was expected at the presidential suite for lunch. The boardroom overlooked a large Chinese garden in a private courtyard. The president had both business and academic connections in China, and the garden showed the Chinese influence, with rows of weeping cherry and peach, an ornamental pond with golden carp and a small faux-Chinese pavilion. In the boardroom a cold lunch was laid out on the table. Wilber and Darian were already there. Mel shook Marcel's hand and greeted him warmly, congratulating him on his new book. He had, he said, seen a write-up in the *New York Review of Books*. After inquiring about enrolments and a prospective new position for the philosophy department, Mel got down to the business at hand, that being Mirielle's role in the new development project. Marcel wondered what this had to do with him, or, at the very least, why Mirielle had not been invited to the lunch. It seemed that Mel wanted to sing Mirielle's praises to Marcel, man to man. Wilber and

Darian were equally enthusiastic.

"We think she will go a *very* long way," Mel intoned, "and we are keen to showcase her talents to the world by way of this project. Actually," he added, "we think her talents might ultimately extend to politics. Such a beautiful woman," he mused fondly. "So sassy, so smart. And hardworking! Ambitious too. Extremely ambitious." Fixing his rather mesmerizing blue gaze on Marcel for a moment, he repeated, thoughtfully, how very, very far Mirielle could go...with the right support....

Marcel was unclear as to Mel's motives, but distinctly uncomfortable. What did Mel want in exchange for the "right support" for Mirielle's "talents"? Did he—did they all—want to sleep with her? But why ask him? They didn't need his permission. Mirielle did what she wanted. So what was it? But Mel had changed tack and was talking about his lodge. He owned a country house, apparently, on a large estate that was set up as a game park, stocked with water fowl, deer and pheasant. It was a kind of private sporting club, as far as Marcel could gather, for a circle of Mel's closest associates, and, it seemed, Marcel was being invited to join them for a weekend at the end of the month. Looking for excuses, Marcel replied hurriedly that he would have to check with Mirielle.

"No, no," Mel said, looking at him meaningfully, his eyes even more protuberant than usual. "This is a *sporting* event— it's not family fun. Even my own wife and beautiful daughters will not be there! It's for men only. Wives would feel out of place. It's a hunting lodge, and in the evening we have male entertainment. We are huge admirers of Mirielle, Marcel, and we want her on the development team. But the hunting lodge is definitely for men only."

Seeing Marcel's reluctance, Mel added slyly, "Guri will be there."

Marcel thanked Mel for the invitation and said he would check his diary. He excused himself from the lunch as quickly as possible and walked disconsolately back to his office through the concrete and steel of the elegantly designed campus. It was clear now that Mirielle's "break" was contingent on this obscure allegiance that Mel was demanding of Marcel. Aware that the "inducements" that Mel had held out the first night—of, what was it? sex with underaged girls?—meant nothing to a man who already possessed every conceivable worldly endowment, and who could turn around and seduce Mel's own step-son just to prove it, Mel had now made Mirielle the target of his lures. This did admittedly make it harder for Marcel. But Mel's proposition was distasteful to him. Such a man had nothing whatever to offer him. But could Marcel afford to risk losing Mirielle?

At home that evening, Marcel did not mention the lunch. Thoroughly spent after a day of teaching, his wife went to bed early, leaving Marcel alone in his study. There were three messages on his red phone, but he did not listen to them. He opened an email from his agent on his laptop and read that two online magazines, a radio station and a television program had requested pre-book release interviews. The news gave him no joy. Restless, his attention wandered. He gazed through the louvered blinds out the study window. There was little to see, only the wall of a neighbouring apartment block. He took down the bird folder again. The paintings and etchings were mostly Chinese, herons and cranes being, of course, the ubiquitous symbol of immortality in Chinese art. But what was immortality? And why was it a crane? Immortality was not, Marcel knew, anything that could be attained through modern medicine or science or cyborg technology or cryonics, all of which would be able at most to add a few decades to the human life span. What on earth was it that these great solitary birds portended? Whatever it was, he was sure he lacked it. And there was in consequence an ache in him, as he gazed at the blank wall of the adjoining apartment block, that nothing in his life at that moment could assuage.

Still at a loss a couple of days later as to how to deal with the president's invitation, Marcel received a text message from Guri. "I think you should come to Ardea's public lecture next week: 'An Ecological Theory of Evil.' Lion Cub." What did Marcel have to lose? Perhaps a dose of ecology was just what he needed, he reflected cynically. Who knew? Ardea was a member of his department after all. Besides, he thought with quiver of warmth, it would be nice to spend an hour or two with Guri. "OK," he texted back, "we'll go together."

It was a lunchtime talk, located in one of the more workaday campus lecture theatres. Only a handful of people were in attendance when Marcel and Guri entered the room. Ardea looked flustered, struggling ineptly with the computer to bring her presentation up on the screen. She did not succeed. The equipment was unresponsive. Even the microphone seemed not to be working. She resigned herself to delivering her talk without technical assistance.

"What is evil?" she began, rather abruptly. "Are there dark essences in human nature, tendencies inherited from our violent, aggressive and territorial primate past? If so, can these tendencies be integrated, through reflexiveness, into a psychological make-up that is morally positive in its overall orientation?" Ardea paused here to explain to her audience that reflexiveness could be understood as our capacity to re-flect upon, evaluate and hence change our own conscious-ness.

"Or perhaps," she continued, "evil is not so much a bio-logical drive, the legacy of our primate past, as a function of our innate need, as social beings, for acceptance and approv-al. Does the self try to gain the existential security that comes with social inclusion by seeking power over others? Does it resort to coercion if it finds it cannot win people's allegiance by sympathetic means…?" Writing up names on a white-board—Plato, Spinoza, Kant, Schopenhauer—Ardea worked her way through a catalogue of classical theories of evil. "Is evil perhaps, as Plato maintained, simply a deficit in under-standing? If we fail to understand the nature of the Good, and hence fail to see that the Good, and only the Good, gen-erates happiness, then do we, out of ignorance, fall into evil?

Kant, of course, concurred at least partially with Plato. The point of life, according to Kant, is not to be happy but *to be worthy of* happiness. It is in choosing to do right that we demonstrate our worthiness, and in choosing worthiness over unworthiness we actualize our essential humanity, which lies in freedom—freedom from the determinism of our own nature and circumstances. To be evil is to be unfree, to be caught in the coils of our conditioning. To be unfree is to be less than human, and for a human being to fail to achieve humanity is to be prey to the deepest discontent."

While Ardea continued for some time to canvas classic accounts of evil, Marcel fidgeted in his seat. Then, coming to the end of her overview, she rubbed the names from the board and declared, with a dramatic little gesture, that she wished to propose a new theory, an *ecological* theory of evil. The key to such a theory, she explained, would be to situate humans, morally speaking, not merely in society but in nature: the entire congregation of life would, from this perspective, constitute our primary moral community. Marcel showed renewed interest. Guri, already absorbed in Ardea's talk, leaned even further forward.

"We live in a natural world," Ardea began, "in which 'evil,' in the sense of the harming and destroying of others, is unavoidable. This is a basic rule of life. We did not invent the rules of life, and we cannot change them. Life feeds on life. Life renews itself at the expense of other living things. This is the biological bottom line, the key to sustenance and regeneration. Yet, as reflexive beings, we humans have the capacity to empathize with the aspiration of all living things to preserve and increase their own existence. With reflexive awareness we can grasp that all living things have an inner life, that they are, like us, centres of sentience, satisfaction, suffering and aspiration. Reflexive awareness creates our capacity for empathy, and empathy gives rise to a sense of the rightness of letting others pursue their own lifeways and the wrongness of thwarting or harming them. Empathy, in other words, gives rise to our moral sense."

"However," Ardea continued, too engrossed now in her

own thought to notice whether the audience was paying attention, "once we recognize the rightness of allowing things to live and blossom and the wrongness of thwarting them, we are in a bind, for the rules of life do require, categorically, that we inflict some harm. Even if we are as kind as we can be—whether to our fellow humans, by following the path of justice, or to our fellow animals, by adopting a compassionate and vegetarian way of life—our very existence impacts on innumerable other beings in a negative manner. We thwart the life-impulse of plants by eating them and exploiting them in countless ways. Plants appropriated by us also represent food taken from the mouths of all manner of other animals. Simply by occupying space in the world, we exclude a host of potential others. And of course, by actively participating in the commercial regimes of modern societies we are, even as vegetarians, implicated in the deaths of legions of creatures: through modern methods of agriculture, forestry, transport, mining and industrial production, for instance, tides of poison are unleashed into ecosystems, habitats are obliterated, fertility is compromised, animals are expunged in daily holocausts of roadkill, medical experimentation, environmental culling—all for our benefit. However, even before modernity began its current large-scale assault on earth's systems, we were, as humans, caught in this existential double bind: on the one hand, we could not avoid causing harm to living things; on the other hand, as far as we allowed ourselves to exercise our reflexivity, we could not help but feel for those things even as we harmed them."

"So," Ardea asked thoughtfully, her attention returning now to her audience, "what to do? We are squirming on a moral hook not of our own making. How are we to escape from it? How are we to resolve the double bind? Well, the default strategy, at least in the Western tradition, has been to treat those we have no recourse but to harm as 'the other.' 'The other' is deemed not to feel, not to share the aspiration to live and prosper that we encounter at first hand in our own subjectivity. The other is deemed not to be a subject, a centre of an inner life, as we are. It is, rather, just an object, all externality, with no existence for itself. As such it cannot matter to itself, hence it does not warrant empathy. No wrongness can attach to harming such an object. We may use it, impair it, destroy it with impunity. There is moreover a logic to this process of 'otherizing' that ensures that the category of 'others' is continually expanded. Suppose that in certain circumstances I find I have to kill an animal to feed my family. I try to reconcile myself to this act, to absolve myself, by 'otherizing' the animal, treating it as an objectified thing with no inner life of any significance or consequence. How can I then avoid extending this otherized status to every animal of the same species? And can there really be any justification for denying an inner life to animals of this species but not to animals of a host of comparable species? Very quickly the act of otherizing will encompass all animal species, and from thence all of nature. And, habituated to denying, for our own moral convenience, the inner life so unmistakably present in other creatures, it may not be long before we are also tempted to deny inner life to classes of humans whom it suits us to exploit or destroy."

"To summarize then," said Ardea, taking a sip of water, "evil arises from a certain tension in our basic existential condition as ecological beings. True, as primates, we have a formidable inheritance of violent and aggressive tendencies. But as primates who also possess a countervailing capacity for reflexivity, we are capable of recognizing the inner life, the subjectivity, of all creatures, and hence of empathizing with them. Empathy can check the violence of our innate tendencies and reveal to us the wrongness of harming others. Even if we overcome our violent tendencies however, we still find ourselves in a moral bind: as ecological beings, we cannot maintain our own existence without hurting others. To exist is to be trapped in a state of moral anguish. In order to escape this trap, we resort to the strategy of otherizing. This elected moral blindness—generally described as anthropocentrism, the incapacity to recognize moral significance in nonhuman life—is preserved by all the dualisms that characterize the Western philosophical tradition, all the human/

nature, culture/nature, mind/body, subject/object, spirit/matter, civilized/primitive type dichotomies that structure our legitimating discourses. It is this self-blinding with respect to living things that is the true root of evil—and I mean by evil not just violence towards nature but the brutality, viciousness and rapaciousness that debase and deprave our relations with one another. To avoid evil, we must acknowledge the moral significance and entitlement to empathy of all life."

"However, if we do acknowledge this while yet sacrificing the nonhuman lives we cannot afford to forego, how are we to preserve our sanity? Ecology itself affords a moral remedy. In ecosystems, living things exact what they need from their fellow beings, but in ways and to a degree that sustains the system overall. Predators, such as wolves, trim the populations of herbivores, such as deer and antelope, so that herbivory does not destroy the grasslands or woodlands on which the entire community of life depends. Death in the right measure is, in an ecological context, a condition for the perpetuation and regeneration of life. So while death remains an evil for the individual, it gains via ecology a second-order meaning as a necessity and indeed a good. In order to escape being trapped existentially in unequivocal evil then we must find that measure—the measure of death that needs to be meted out by us in order to sustain the larger flourishing of life. This is a kind of pre-moral *Law*," Ardea paused here to exchange glances with Guri, "that must be discovered anew in every ecological context. In earlier times, hunter-gatherer societies were often organized around exquisitely accurate reckonings of the exact proportions of necessary death. But in the industrialized societies of today, our grasp of the correct proportionalities is lost. We have to re-discover these proportionalities, not from indigenous baselines, but from the perspective of contemporary realities. In most modern societies, for example, animals need no longer be killed for meat. Vegetarian options exist. Carnivory on our part is no longer required. Since it is also in flagrant contradiction to compassion, it lacks a contemporary moral basis. But reconfiguring our food desires is just the beginning. A transvaluation of all desires is required if we are to re-discover that primal, pre-moral Law. All our desires have to be reconfig-ured to avoid direct harm to living things unless such harm is truly a condition for the larger community of life. Even in cases where harm is such a condition, complacency is not excusable. Acquiesce though we may in grave necessities that transcend compassion, we are still bound, as reflexive beings, to feel and regret the suffering of those who are sacrificed."

"Please don't underestimate the reach of my argument," Ardea exclaimed, challenging her audience. "I'm suggesting not only that anthropocentrism is inadequate as a basis for environmental ethics but that it is the root of evil itself. Full stop. Ethics is premised on empathy for all living things. Yes, we might find limited outbreaks of inter-tribal violence in hunter-gatherer societies that do indeed respect and revere nature, but such outbreaks will usually be in response to transient issues that endanger the stability or survival of the group. Generally speaking, when living things, in and of themselves, are honoured, when every insect is treated with respect and only killed if its death is truly necessary in the larger scheme of things, then violence amongst humans will be minimal."

"On the other hand, when people 'otherize' nature in or-der to justify cannibalizing the rest of life, laying waste to it, systematically and on a grand scale, as is happening in the current regime of global development, empathy and hence ethics will unravel. Epic violence amongst peoples and na-tions is guaranteed to ensue. There is a certain poetic justice in this," Ardea concluded sadly. "The moral logic that allows us to arrogate to ourselves a biosphere that rightfully belongs to all species is bound to unleash end-times violence amongst ourselves. Thank you."

The lecture was received with perfunctory applause then people quickly dispersed. Ardea also hurriedly vacated the scene. Marcel remained in his seat. Guri was looking at him, waiting for him to speak.

"It was bold," Marcel conceded. "And not bad. Environ-mental philosophy is not my field, but philosophy of evil is.

What she had to say was, hmm, novel."

Marcel's tone was stiff and Guri suspected little of what it cost him to make this concession. Used to re-working the history of ideas in his elegant, erudite yet popular presentations and accustomed to receiving accolades for learnedness rather than for first-hand thinking, Marcel preferred not to dwell on the topic of originality. But here, face to face with someone attempting to think through an existential issue from scratch, it was galling to be reminded that, for all his success, he was not himself such a thinker.

"Yes, quite novel," he repeated lifelessly. "Though simplistic. Naïve. And woefully deficient in scholarship."

"Aha, I knew it!" Guri whispered, undeterred. "She's brilliant!"

Marcel loosened up and laughed, cuffing Guri with a mock lion paw. Guri ducked, and laughed back up at him with pleasure.

When Marcel left the campus early that evening he had two conundrums to ponder. First was the conundrum of the president's invitation. To accept it was to compromise himself but to refuse it was to risk alienating Mirielle. But now there was also Ardea. How could someone so insignificant be in possession of something that, he sensed, eluded him? How, more importantly, could he take it from her?

The following day Marcel sprang into action. From his desk in the philosophy department he sent a message to the president's office accepting the invitation, though he had no intention of attending the event. He would find an excuse closer to the time. Having temporarily settled that matter he strode down the corridor to Ardea's door and knocked. She called to enter, but was startled when she saw him there, having been left in no uncertainty as to his erstwhile lack of interest in her

"I enjoyed your lecture yesterday," he told her, "and

wanted to congratulate you. The work you are doing on evil is extraordinary! I wonder," he hazarded, "if you would care to join me in the staff club today for lunch? I'd love to hear more about your ideas."

Ardea, surprised, was instantly flattered. She was not unaware of the value of her work; she recognized the originality of her thought and the depth and importance of her field of research. She did not however expect colleagues like Marcel to recognize it. She said she'd be delighted to lunch with him but that today she had scheduled a postgraduate supervision in the midday slot. Besides, she admitted, she didn't really care for the staff club. Tomorrow she would be downtown at a planning meeting with a group called Sea Watch. Might he possibly be free to lunch with her there? She knew a café on a cliff-top overlooking the bay that was a good place to blow away the cobwebs of the academy!

Marcel agreed, though inwardly resenting the rescheduling such a sortie off-campus would entail. The next day however, as he drove across to the beach, he was glad she had made him depart from his routine. It was a glorious morning, and he chose an outside table at the little café; from this high perch he surveyed, on either side, a spectacular line of coast. While he breathed in the salt breeze, his taut mind relaxed and expanded out into a vastness of blue. When Ardea arrived she was wrapped in a towel and wearing a one-piece swimsuit, her hair wet. She laughed and apologized, and said she'd just had time for a dip. Without sitting down she rushed off to the bathroom to dress, re-emerging after a minute in jeans and tee-shirt.

Marcel had planned to move into seduction mode, or at least to set up the preliminaries. If he was going to crack the enigma that Ardea had now become for him he would have to get to know her well. But it was difficult to find a seductive pitch with the sea breeze whipping his words away, forcing him to raise his voice. Sunlight was glancing everywhere off water, metal and glass, creating a wall of dazzle between the two of them. He had to content himself with asking her, entirely conventionally, about herself and how she had become interested in ecology. He drew out too her views on the environmental crisis, and encouraged her to explain how she thought an environmental ethic—that respected the rights of all natural beings and systems to live and blossom in their own way—could ever gain enough acceptance in modern society to slow the headlong advance of capitalism that was demolishing everything in its path. Marcel asked these questions out of politeness, without real interest, but Ardea responded with intensity, which bored Marcel, who had to stifle a yawn or two in the course of the conversation. It was not that Ardea was boring. Far from it. Everything she said was freshly minted, vibrant with the movement of engaged thought. But it was, regardless, boring for Marcel to be with any woman who was either insufficiently attractive to interest him or too serious about the topic of their conversation to flirt with him.

As Ardea had made her way to the beach that morning by public transport, Marcel was now able to offer her a lift back to campus. In the intimate and expensive interior of his black Porsche, Marcel felt confident to try a line.

"Tell me, Ardea," he began, as the car slipped into the traffic....She looked around at him quickly. "Forgive me for asking...," he hesitated, "...but, are you happy?"

Ardea's eyes widened. "Am I happy? Well...," she pondered, then returned truthfully, "...I suppose not."

Marcel felt a little thrill of relief. He had not imagined she could be happy, but was gratified to hear her actually confirm it. It meant she possessed no secret that was beyond his reach.

"Are you at all...depressed then," he asked, a tad too complacently.

"No!" she exclaimed. "No, not at all! Why should I be depressed?"

"You just said you weren't happy," Marcel rejoined.

"Yes, but of course that doesn't mean I'm *un*happy."

"Oh, you're content then," Marcel mumbled, instantly losing interest.

"No!" cried Ardea, regaining her intensity. "Anything but content!" Marcel looked at her with curiosity.

"What then?" he asked.

She hunted around for words. "You could say I'm…um …*full.*"

"Full," Marcel repeated. "As in, fulfilled?"

"Not exactly…I have none of the things that fulfill. And yet, I am…not empty. I am the opposite of empty! So I suppose that means I am…er…full."

"Full of what?" Marcel asked.

"Well," Ardea faltered, "I don't know. That's not the right question. When I said I was full I was thinking of how I can sit on the porch and just gaze and gaze. At the sky. At the clouds. At the birds that come to the birdbaths in my garden. I like to watch them. Actually, I like to know all about them—I like to identify them, check who's around, who's nesting where, who's arrived and who's left the neighbourhood. I like to look at the trees, at which ones are flowering, who's pollinating the flowers, who's eating the pollinators, that kind of thing. Just sitting on the porch or filling the birdbaths or puttering around in the vegetable patch gives me so much joy…it can be *enough* for me."

"But surely," Marcel interjected, "that *can't* be enough! What do you *live for*? What do you *desire*?"

Flustered, Ardea coloured. "Well, I guess I want what everyone wants. I want love. Maybe a family. I want a decent career. Enough money to live on. I want friends. I want to have time to write and for my writing to be read and appreciated….I want all of that. And those are the things that make me happy. When I don't get those things, I'm sometimes sad. But none of that is what I *live for*. I live for the other things— the birds and what not…." She gestured vaguely.

Marcel, slipping into the overtaking lane, murmured sceptically, "I'm sure that can't be enough."

Ardea paused. "Well, you're right. It's not enough just to observe the world. One also has to *sing* it. To *sing back*, to *answer* the song."

Marcel straightened in his seat, not taking his eyes off the road.

"But what if everything goes wrong in your life? If you lose your job, become poor and abandoned? Will singing the world sustain you? What if no-one hears your song?"

Ardea cringed slightly. "If everything goes wrong in my life—and I admit that, in our society, that's what is quite likely to happen to someone like me—then I'll give up and die, like anyone else. But still, singing the world is what I will have lived for. And nothing and no one can stop me doing it. The birds and things are always there. I only have to open my eyes and step outside, step into the song. So no, I'm not and never will be depressed."

Marcel looked away, disconcerted.

"And you," Ardea broke off. "Are you happy?"

"Yes, I am," he shrugged, also speaking truthfully. "Very happy. I've got everything I could possibly want. I have a stunning wife, a luxury apartment. I just have to wave my credit card like a magic wand and anything I want materializes in front of me. Critics like my books; students like my classes. I have no end of academic projects and intellectual goals to which I can look forward. I count famous and influential people amongst my friends. I even have a Porsche," he smiled, and kept smiling slightly, thinking of other gratifications he was too well-bred to mention.

"And?" Ardea asked shrewdly.

"And what?" he replied evenly, glancing at her.

"Are you depressed?"

He stared at her for a few moments, then, looking back to the road, stated simply, flatly, "Yes. I am very happy, and I am depressed."

"And I," she exclaimed, rather too buoyantly, "am not happy, and not depressed."

They exchanged glances again, she triumphantly, he discomfited.

"You are a very strange person, Ardea," he said, shutting down their game of truth-or-dare and returning abruptly to convention.

The next morning Marcel found a voice message from Ardea on his phone at work. She had been thinking about their conversation, she said, and suspected he would probably only ever get a feel for environmental ethics through experience. She knew a very special place, not too far away, she'd be happy to take him, if he were so inclined. Marcel was indeed so inclined! Though more for the sake of understanding Ardea than for the sake of appreciating environmental ethics. Mirielle had a faculty retreat that very weekend, as it happened. He quickly phoned Ardea to see if they could arrange the trip then.

The following Saturday accordingly found the two of them in each other's company once more, this time in Ardea's battered four wheel drive, heading for a secluded mangrove swamp that had been Ardea's playground, she told Marcel, since childhood. They drove down off the escarpment, where Westin College was located, to a low plain. As they wended through woodland and open fields, Ardea, to Marcel's dismay, pulled over a couple of times to drag roadkill out of the path of traffic.

"I do it as a mark of respect," she explained.

To his grimace when she stopped to pick up an already bloodied racoon, she explained that carcasses attracted other animals onto the roadway, where they in turn would become victims. Unable to argue with this, Marcel merely looked away.

After an hour or so they arrived in marshier terrain. Soon they were inside thick bushland laced everywhere with brackish canals and inlets. Ardea drove straight to a small harbour in the midst of a tall mangrove forest. There was a boating cabin by the beach, and in front of it, a wooden jetty, where rowboats were lashed. She took a key from the glove box, opened the cabin, and fetched some oars. Handing a pair to Marcel she retrieved a large pack and some waders from the back of the vehicle and scrambled into one of the boats. Marcel followed. Ardea pushed off and then proceeded to navigate the boat expertly through a labyrinth of channels that crisscrossed shallow mangrove flats studded with little cypress and pine islands. Marcel had never been amongst mangroves before, and marvelled at the enchanted ambience created by the arches and flying buttresses of their high exposed roots. The canopy covered the channels, so although they were afloat they were also inside a grotesque and fantastical woodland, a liminal, dreamy zone between normal waking categories. The play of light and shadow lifting off the tarnished water was also hypnotic, and Marcel found himself growing drowsy, despite the exertion of rowing. Occasionally they passed through open tidal pools, invariably full of wading birds that took flight at their approach. Ardea identified the birds for him: cormorants, moorhens, herons, ibis, brown pelicans. A couple of times, to Ardea's delight, they rowed past a sea turtle, visible in every detail in the clear water, its head protruding, its neck raised at right angles to its body. She also pointed out trees and plants as they proceeded: red alder, hemlock, spruce.

Eventually they came to a larger island. Ardea tied the boat to a mangrove root, rolled up her jeans, handed the pack to Marcel and led the way over a natural deck of tangled woody roots, vines and other vegetation till they reached firm ground. Here the woods were thicker and darker, but there was a path and Ardea followed it. They came out into a large clearing, a natural grassland inside a horseshoe of cypress and pine that opened at its far end onto a tidal pool. At that far end was a cabin which, Ardea explained, served as a bird hide. They made their way across to the solid log structure with its large window on the pool side and, behind, a fireplace. Marcel wandered down to the water's edge, while Ardea built a fire and produced supplies and utensils from her pack. Before long she called him back and they sat down to a lunch of spinach pie and steaming tea.

The transformation in Ardea was plain to see. Here, in her element, she was vibrant and relaxed. Her hesitancy had vanished and her competence was, to Marcel, impressive. She chattered happily, explaining aspects of the natural history of the place, how the islands had been formed and why mangrove systems are sites of such intense fecundity. She also called up memories from her childhood, how they had camped on this island in the summers, how her father and brothers had fished and crabbed and she had filled book after book with drawings of ibis, egret, pelican and crane.

"I'd love to see those drawings one day," Marcel murmured.

She remembered how they had all outdone one another, around the campfire, telling tales of mangrove ghosts and spiteful shrimp fairies. She recalled too how she had once, as a small child, become accidentally stranded on the island and had spent the night in a tree, for fear of alligators. There were moments when, alone under the lilting canopies, she had felt the world open to her—what was "outside," she said, would assume an uncanny, ethereal aspect, as if she were experiencing it from within the psychic interiority of the world itself. In those moments, she explained, it was as if she had slipped under the skin of the world, and everything, including herself, took on a fluid, numinous dreamlikeness. During those moments, she mused, one could feel the flow of psychic arising—as if everything were charged with *streaming*, the streaming inherent in *psychic* process, an aspect of reality that is not manifest when things are observed merely under their outer aspect.

Gazing at Ardea, Marcel leaned back on the sand, locking his hands behind his head.

"Environmentalists are always talking about *oneness, interconnectedness*," he ventured, smiling, "but I've never been able to see the point of that. If the purpose of our existence is to become blended back into some kind of original unity, why were we created in the first place? I mean, why did the

Unity self-differentiate into individual things if the point of individual existence is just to return to Unity—to sink back into undifferentiated wholeness? Surely, since reality did self-differentiate, the point of our existence is to fully realize ourselves as individuals?"

"Oh philosophers!" Ardea laughed, pushing gently at his chest. "You tell them your deepest, most precious and private secret and they disagree with it!"

Her hair was a mess, there was dirt under her fingernails and sweat on her collar, but as she had been talking her face had been alive, her expressions melting into one another, her eyes bold and warm. Even as he challenged her, Marcel was charmed. Yes, he had felt, momentarily, the magic of the mangrove forest, the pull towards a dreamier, more timeless zone, and yes, he could appreciate the extraordinary fecundity of this place, where land and sea slipped in and out of each other, like a primal scene of procreation. But he was more moved by the shift in Ardea. She had blossomed indeed, not in response to him but in response to this place, to this homeland of life itself, where the very atmosphere, hushed and still as it was, breathed, and all beings, from the tiniest crustacean to the majestic white egret and the deer that lurked on the islands, were locked into a single tidal rhythm, a single net of wavering light, an encompassing dream.

"Still," he continued, with smiling insistence, "it's a problem, isn't it? I really can't see the point of mysticism. The universe has given us our existence as individual beings. Surely, if it 'wants' anything at all, it's that we make the most of that existence, that we live our individual lives to the full, refusing to be hemmed in by arbitrary credos. Why seek to blend ourselves back into the undifferentiated...?"

Ardea paused, drew up her knees, wrapped her arms around them, then, resting her face sideways on her forearms, returned Marcel's gaze.

"Well, Marcel," she began, "don't ask me for the metaphysics. I only know there's a joy to be had, a discovery to be made, when you wake up to all the lives around you—when you become immersed in them, not just as an observer but as a participant, protecting and providing for them, yes, but also walking amongst them, as it were, experiencing what it is like to be vulnerable to them, encountering their resistance. When you really become immersed in the life around you, when you know it in all its particularity, and you're not just an observer but a participant, engaged, in deadly earnest, in the push and pull of it, then something happens...It *is* as though the world opens, and you step through the veil of appearance, right into the midst of the real, which is this streaming thing, this fluid thing, in which energy and meaning are mixed, and directions, pathways, open at your feet...."

Marcel reached over and took her hand.

"Thank you, Ardea," he said simply. "I believe you though I haven't the slightest idea what the experience you're describing would feel like."

Ardea cupped her other hand over his and sighed. "It's about contact with the real," she replied. "Only by opening out to the life around us, and aligning with it, do we experience the real. When we treat the life around us as mere backdrop, then everything remains unreal. Including our own selves. Anyway," she brightened, unclasping her hands and getting to her feet, "Guri has figured it out. Ask him about it!"

After packing up the lunch things they explored the island. Although pleased and enlivened, Marcel was also keeping an anxious eye on the tide. Wouldn't it be harder to navigate once the pools were high? When Ardea suggested they take a swim in the pool, Marcel asked whether they had enough time. Ardea settled another long look on him. Then she turned away, and, humming to herself, embarked on a little made-up song, while rapidly and purposefully shedding her clothes:

When God made time, he made
Plenty of it
Plenty of it
Plenty of it,

When God made time, he made
Plenty of it,
So don't tell me there's no time.

At the last line she turned back to Marcel and laughed up at him so unaffectedly and infectiously, despite her nudity, that Marcel relaxed, whipped off his own clothes, and followed her into the water. As they dipped and splashed, Marcel asked, hesitantly, whether they might stay the night on the island rather than try to navigate the tide? Ardea faltered momentarily but then laughed again, this time for sheer pleasure. Later, on the beach, he inquired whether they had food for the night. "Yes," she replied. She had brought supplies in case of emergencies. There were blankets in a tin chest inside the cabin and an old iron bed. It was rough, but the necessities were there. Marcel felt a stirring of real excitement— something he could not remember experiencing for many a year. He reached out to Ardea and again gently took her hand.

"It's your call," he said to her softly, "you're the boss of the island."

"Okay," she said. "Let's gather wood for the fire."

By sunset their preparations for the night were complete. Ardea had found a jar of honey in an old cupboard in the cabin.

"Food of the immortals," she beamed.

"Why?" asked Marcel.

"Honey is sterile," she answered. "Bacteria can't live in it so it can't decompose. In a sealed container it will last forever!"

Now they sat on the beach overlooking the pool, mugs of tea and honey in hand. They were sitting close. The blaze of an extravagant sunset transfigured not only the sky but the water before them, where wading birds still fished and a few pelicans sailed.

"Look!" exclaimed Ardea suddenly, pointing upwards. A magnificent white bird had appeared overhead. It circled a couple of times before alighting on a pine-top at the far end of the pool. As it did so, Ardea leapt to her feet and ran forward. A white feather was floating delicately, turning around and around in slow motion, towards the ground. She dived on it as it landed and clutching it joyfully, returned to Marcel's side.

"It's the great white heron," she cried. "You're so lucky to have seen it, Marcel!"

Marcel remarked that he thought he'd seen the same bird a number of times that day.

"Oh no," said Ardea. "That was the white egret. Also a beautiful bird. But the great white heron is different. It's a rare morph of the great blue heron, and is normally found only in southern Florida. But there's a breeding pair of great white herons here. It's probably the only breeding pair north of Florida. When they're seen at all outside their range it's usually just as lone wanderers. Hardly anyone is aware of the breeding pair here. Great whites are so elusive. I discovered their nesting place years ago and still check on them from time to time, but it's been ages since I've actually seen one abroad like this. I can't believe it's visited us tonight!"

Marcel put his arm around her shoulders and touched his cheek to hers.

"You're a very special person, Ardea," he said softly.

That evening Ardea draped mosquito netting over the old iron bedstead they had carried out onto the beach. She cushioned the rusty wire mesh with a thermal bedroll and blanket from the tin chest. The night was warm, moonlit. They lay down, swathed themselves in netting and turned to face each other. Marcel saw Ardea's eyes dilate as she tried to adjust to the sudden proximity, the sudden loss of space between them. Whose was this fleshy slab of cheek and crumpled eye pressed up against her, he imagined her thinking, these pudgy fingers on her arm? Where was "Marcel"? Where was her own solidity? From the glazing over of her face it was clear she was suddenly, privately, in free fall. Her body had stiffened, her bones, knees, digging into him. He drew back a little, any desire that might have been kindling instantly extinguished. But this was a threshold over which he had eased many women. Patience would be needed. She had earlier fastened the heron's feather to one of the bedposts so he reached up for it and, with its tip, began to stroke her face. Half smiling, he asked her about men, her father, her brothers, had she ever been in love? Gradually she relaxed. And what about her mother, he queried. Her mother had died when she was very young. As they chatted, he traced her eyebrows, cheeks, shoulders. By tickling her nose he made her laugh. When he judged she had retrieved herself, he let the feather wander over the rest of her body, following its curves, investigating its hollows with a touch as light as breath. Calm now, Ardea opened like a flower to the morning sun. Quietly and tenderly, without haste or lust, as a continuation of their conversation, Marcel made love to her, keeping to the slow rhythm of the place, where land and sea breathed eternally, in and out of each other. It was kind and tender, more like a book at bedtime than the karma sutra, and afterwards she snuggled into him happily, as trusting as a puppy. Like babes in the wood, he thought to himself wonderingly.

When Mirielle arrived home the following night, after her weekend staff retreat, Marcel told her, in abridged form, of the field trip with his strange colleague and his induction into the mysteries of environmental ethics via the visitation of the great white heron. Disregarding the implied infidelity, Mirielle asked him the exact location of the swamp. Marcel mapped out for her the route that Ardea had taken. Mirielle cried out with exasperation.

"Don't you realize that's the Wilkins Heng-Hu site," she almost shrieked. "That's the inland end of the estuary we're about to drain! And you've been fraternizing with the enemy and having mystical experiences in it! Oh my God," she groaned, rolling her eyes. "I don't believe it, Marcel."

Marcel was himself stunned. He hadn't realized they had been in an estuary. In any case, surely a wonderland of such obviously high conservation value had some kind of environmental protection?

"Yes," Mirielle conceded, "but all protection is reversible. They've found gas under the marshes and the economic arguments for extraction will outweigh the arguments for conservation, and development will be tied in the first phase to the extraction project. When the gas hub has compromised the conservation values of the area, the second phase of the development will kick in. It will be argued on economic grounds and by then the economic values will outweigh the conservation values. That's standard procedure," Mirielle remarked impatiently. "Everybody knows the drill." She added that the applications for the mining permit and for infrastructure development had been finalized and were, as it happened, about to be lodged in the next day or two.

Marcel said nothing.

"While we're on the subject," Mirielle, suppressing her irritation, forged on, "I meant to ask if you had accepted Mel's invitation yet?"

"To the hunting party?"

"Yes," said Mirielle. "The party is in two weeks time."

"Yes, I have," Marcel shrugged. "But I have no intention of going."

"What do you mean?" Mirielle exclaimed, her voice rising almost to shrillness again. "You know how important it is for me that you go!"

"But Mirielle, I don't shoot. I detest the very idea of hunting."

"Why?" Mirielle retorted. "Why is this such a big production? You eat meat, don't you? Venison? Pheasant, maybe in a restaurant? Why shouldn't you kill what you eat yourself? Why should you let other people do the dirty work for you?"

Marcel smiled faintly at Mirielle's sudden interest in philosophical argument.

"Maybe so," he said, "but eating meat doesn't mean I should *enjoy* killing things, that I should engage in it as *sport*. Consenting to kill out of necessity and enjoying killing for its own sake, as recreation, are two entirely different things. And in any case, shooting is not the only sport on the agenda. What about the fourteen year old girls?"

"Oh, spare me the sermon," Mirielle rejoined impatiently. "And the philosophizing. You don't have to do anything you don't want to, and besides, since when have you been squeamish about sex? Mel will have covered himself against any risk of prosecution."

Slightly stunned again, Marcel drew back.

"You really, seriously want me to go," he said slowly.

"Yes, Marcel, I do. Really, seriously. There is a great deal at stake for me—for us—and I want you to stand by me."

Alarmed at Mirielle's implied ultimatum, Marcel did not knock on Ardea's door for the next few days. Mid-week however Guri dropped into his office with the news that in class that day Ardea had been distraught. The Onaway estuary was, apparently, threatened with development.

"It's where she grew up," Guri said breathlessly. "She was terribly upset. Sea Watch, the organization she's associated with, is going to lead a campaign against the development. June and I have both signed the petition. We're planning to join the campaign."

Marcel sighed, and thanked Guri for letting him know.

"You're the head of her department," Guri reminded him. "No-one here supports her. I think you should stand up for her."

In bed that night, Mirielle told Marcel that she had mentioned to Mel the incident of the great white heron.

"Mel was flabbergasted," she added, "that you were out there with Ardea. He despises her, and I had to cover up for you. I said you were looking for a way to get rid of her—that you thought if you could get to the bottom of the activities of that extremist group she's associated with—Sea Watch—you might find grounds for dismissing her. Apparently she's been radicalizing her students. Mel was all for bringing terrorist charges against her."

Marcel raised himself on his elbow and stared at Mirielle in disbelief.

"Ardea is a small-time environmentalist," he said, making an effort to keep his voice steady. "She's a harmless romantic and doesn't have a political bone in her body."

"Well," Mirielle spat back spitefully, "I guess you would know what's inside her body. Anyway," she added, "romantics are the most dangerous types, the most fanatical." She paused for a moment. "Are you in love with her?"

"In love with her!" Marcel exploded. "(a) I am not an adolescent who falls in love with people; and (b) I have a wife like the queen of Sheba who just about blows the top off my head every night. What would I want with a little countercultural mouse like Ardea?"

"That's just as well," Mirielle retorted, "because you're going to have to prize out of her the location of her precious heron's nesting site. You said she knows. The great white heron is a rare bird. It's iconic. Its presence in the estuary could be a major stumbling block for the development. It'll have to be removed."

Mirielle turned her back on Marcel, who slumped onto his pillow, eyes wide open.

Later that week Mirielle was invited to a downtown dinner with Mel, Darian and Wilber. Since talk would be shop, Mel suggested, via Mirielle, that Marcel not join them till after-dinner drinks. So it was fairly late in the evening when Marcel arrived at the entrance to an expensive club at the business end of town. As a waiter ushered him in, he caught a glimpse, at the far end of the discreetly lit room, of Mirielle in a booth with the three men. She was flushed and laughing, leaning back, her breasts almost entirely escaping the clasp of her low-cut dress. The men were leaning in towards her eagerly, also laughing, and her flesh glimmered like a candle lamp in the semi-darkness. Marcel stopped, inwardly gasping, taking in the scene. His wife was indeed a queen of Sheba, he realized, more beautiful and more sexually numinous than any mortal had a right to be. A queen of Sheba must have her gold mines, must have her throne, her courtiers and admirers. A jolt of pain shot through him as he saw Mel take her hand in both of his then slowly pass it on to each of the other men, while Mirielle bestowed her laughingly inviting smile on each of them in turn. They looked up then, and saw him. Mirielle called delightedly to him, unabashed. He knew, as he walked towards the table, that he would have to keep her, whatever the cost.

Armed with this resolve, Marcel left a message for Ardea the following day. It was almost a week since their night on the island. Ardea had caught sight of him at the far end of corridors once or twice, but hearing no word was wondering anxiously about the state of his feelings. Would she meet with him that evening, he asked in text. She sighed. There were assignments to mark, lectures to prepare. But such was her anxiety, she immediately replied, yes.

That evening, Marcel drove to Ardea's home in woodlands well out of town. The house, in an isolated setting, was picturesque in a rustic way though a little in need of repair. Solar panels glinted from the roof and rainwater tanks fed birdbaths and ponds placed strategically around the site. A sprawling garden with a vegetable plot and fruit trees backed onto forest. A small white dog met him at the gate, barking. It rushed at him as he entered, and he looked around, alarmed. Ardea appeared on the porch, laughing, and called the dog off. Wild ravens sat contentedly in a row along the porch railing, unfazed by Ardea's presence. Discomforted, Marcel followed Ardea into the living room. Amongst a jumble of antique and secondhand furnishings, Ardea cleared a space for him and stationed herself opposite, a wall of books behind her. She offered him a glass of wine and poured a large one for herself. Marcel winced inwardly. This was going to be a long evening. But he mustered his charm and outwardly assumed an ingratiating air. Ardea, relieved to have him seek her out at all, was in no mind to detect the fraud. Her own heart had been in turmoil since the night they had spent together, her worst fear being that he would simply dump her. Now she chattered nervously, taking him into her homespun world confidingly, though aware of the fragility of her every move.

Marcel was accustomed to feigning romantic interest in women, so it was not too difficult for him to hint at feelings he did not possess, or at long-term intimacies he had no intention of bringing to pass. He spoke of an epiphany he had experienced on the island, a shift in his sensibilities.

"I've been depressed for years," he confessed again. "But now I can see the possibility of a new life, a new departure."

He left unsaid but hanging in the air the thought that that life might be with her.

"But what about your wife," Ardea blurted out nervously.

"Oh," Marcel gestured offhandedly, "Mirielle knows I need a long leash."

Ardea gazed back at him impassively. Without admitting it, she felt she would be happy to have him in her life on any terms. She could barely grasp that he might consider leaving his glamorous wife for her. That he was interested in her at all struck her as astonishing, but, undaunted and unquestionably flattered, she soldiered on through the situation. Gone entirely was the naturalness and ease of their enchanted night, when he had gilded every inch of her body with the great white feather. Sensing her panic, Marcel felt a pang of remorse. There was more authenticity in the crook of Ardea's little finger than in the whole of his big celebrity self, he knew. It was she whom the immortal bird had entrusted with its secret. It was she to whom the world revealed its infinitely vulnerable beauty, and it was she who received that beauty rapturously, storing it where it belonged, in the human heart. He should have been kneeling at her feet, but here she was, flustered and anxious, offering herself up for sexual sacrifice.

Abruptly, weary of his own charm and the susceptibility of others to it, he dropped his façade and patted the sofa beside him.

"Come and sit with me," he said in a more down-to-earth tone.

She joined him and he put his arm around her.

"Ardea," he said, "forget everything I just said to you. I'm not in love with you. I love my wife. But you mean something to me, something I don't yet understand myself. You have something I need, something deeply missing from my life, and I'll admit I wanted to take it from you. But I no longer want to do that. Actually, I can no longer bear to do that. To take it from you would be precisely to destroy the possibility that I could ever have it for myself. You are so defenceless," he mused, starting to stroke her hair, "yet you also seem so. . . indestructible." Hesitantly, Ardea leaned her head against his shoulder, letting down her guard a little. "So," Marcel went on, "something is changing in me, and I don't yet know what it is, and I can't promise anything. I do love my wife, but you also have a place in my heart, a real and tender place, which I don't yet know how to name."

He kissed the top of her head and looked down at her for a moment, while she returned his gaze wonderingly, with dawning happiness.

"But," Marcel continued, twisting slightly in his seat, "there is something I need to ask you. I came here tonight with the intention of tricking you into giving me certain information. But now I find I can't do that. I just have to ask you to give it to me freely out of whatever feeling you may have for me. And I have to ask you to trust that I need the information very badly, or I would never ever ask you for it."

Ardea continued to gaze at him, but now her eyes were troubled. "What do you need to know," she whispered, with a sudden chilling intimation.

Marcel whispered, even lower, "I need to know...the location, the nesting site, in the estuary of your friends, you know, the herons, the great white herons...."

Ardea leapt from the couch, her eyes instantly blazing.

"I will never tell you that, Marcel," she exclaimed, outraged. "Never! How could you ask me!" There was no longer any uncertainty in her tone as she declared, "It's best that you go!"

Taken aback, Marcel rose from the couch and followed Ardea out of the room. As she stood on the veranda watching him walk to the gate, the little white dog yapping at his heels, tears of both anger and grief welled in her eyes. She walked back into her kitchen to face the long night, and all the long nights to come. She had to stoop over the table, clutching its sides, as her heart convulsed with disappointment.

The weekend of the lodge party was drawing near. Marcel had explained to Mirielle that Ardea had refused to divulge the nesting site of the great white heron. Mirielle had said nothing but passed the information on to Mel. It was clear she expected Marcel to play his part convincingly at the lodge. Not that she expected him actually to shoot. He had never handled a gun in his life. But she insisted that he accept Mel's invitation to become part of the inner circle. Her own future, she sensed, depended on this.

Marcel texted Guri to ask if he was planning to attend the event, but to his dismay Guri did not reply, disapproving of Marcel's failure to support Ardea's fight for the estuary. Guri had now become aware that his step-father was a driving force behind the Onaway development, so his involvement in the campaign was covert, but all the more passionate for that reason. Marcel wondered what would happen when Mel found out that Guri was supporting Ardea. He feared for the lion cub. Would Mel seek to bring terrorist charges against his stepson?

Soon the day of the hunting party arrived. Mirielle had been a little aloof since Marcel had failed to extract the secret of the nesting site from Ardea. She too, he thought bitterly, was no doubt disillusioned with him. So it was in a bleak mood that he drove out along the winding hedge-lined roads that led through golf links, new housing estates and private game parks to the dreaded destination. He noticed he was not unaware of roadkill as he passed, deer outstretched in holocaustal postures, unremarked, foxes split from head to tail by heedless tires. Ardea, he thought grimly, had left her mark on him.

The lodge was set on undulating ground, fifteen hundred acres in area, abounding in woods and wetlands. Marcel caught sight of a large flock of waterfowl on a lake as he drove to the house. He was greeted at the entrance by Mel himself, who bustled him genially into a reception hall, where thirty or so men were already mingling. They included academics and senior administrators from the university but also, Marcel was surprised to note, senior staff from the corporate world, including several Chinese men, as well as a sprinkling of politicians. Mel introduced him to a small group, where Marcel was asked about his shooting prowess. Impeccably cool and composed, despite his inner misgivings, Marcel made light of his inexperience. Mel laughed sardonically, though his intense blue gaze, hooded by occasional slow, intentional blinks, expressed no hint of irony.

"Marcel is becoming a bit of an environmentalist," he quipped. "But *we* are the real environmentalists, are we not," he declared pointedly. "We cull the wildfowl and deer in order to manage their populations. Without our efforts, all the species on this estate would be in trouble. They'd over-breed, over-graze, and in no time at all their populations, and the entire system, would crash." The men in the small group laughed.

"That's right, Mel," one of them agreed, "we're all environmentalists now."

After lunch, the men donned army fatigues and, shouldering semi-automatic weapons, headed out in large four-wheel drive vehicles to selected sites on the property. One half went to woodlands to shoot deer, hare, pheasant and quail, while the other half went to marshy wetlands to shoot waterfowl. Marcel found himself in the group with Mel, bound for the wetlands. Mel was trying to persuade him to select a weapon. "Give it a go," he was exhorting. Continuing his earlier theme, he insisted—again with a sardonic smile— that hunting was the *real* nature experience. Hunters hunted in order to experience the wild, not just as scenery, but as part of their own nature. They wanted to be stretched, challenged, pushed to their limits. "Only hunters," he said, "tracking prey through thick scrub, really enter wilderness, flow out into it with all their senses. Greenies know nothing about nature," he added derisively. "They want to rescue things, put them in pens, tuck them up in hospital beds. My own son," he added, eyes momentarily glassing with suppressed fury, "has succumbed to green zealotry. He's become vegetarian and has pin-ups of slaughtered animals—martyrs, he calls them—all over his bedroom wall. He's wasting his time, I tell him, treating animal deaths as tragedies. Nature is a death camp, not a teddy bear hospital. To respect and emulate nature is to kill, without fear or favour. Greenies are sickeningly sentimental, always talking about being one with nature, when every hunter knows it's in the moment of the kill, when one looks into the victim's eyes, that one experiences a sense of oneness with it."

Marcel, alarmed at Mel's remark concerning Guri, allowed the president to deliver his sarcastic little lecture, but when they arrived at the wetland and the men disembarked and arrayed themselves for battle, he saw just how mocking the soliloquy had been. There was no physical extremis or mystical communion in the adventure, no tracking or need for heightened senses. The men crept down to the water's edge and opened fire on a peaceful flock of wild geese and ibis in the semi-distance. Since they were using semi-automatic weapons it was simply a massacre. Servants in waders were dispatched to collect the bodies of the birds. Marcel was disgusted. The men climbed back into the vehicles, beer cans in hand, and drove to the next wetland, where the performance was repeated. A dull, tasteless and violent pastime, as Marcel had expected.

At dinner in the Lodge that evening trestles groaned with roasted fowl from the day's slaughter, each bird presented whole, adorned with plumage. Mel sermonized again from the head of the table about the need for meat-eaters to have the moral courage to kill their own food, and about the organic and environmental virtues of game. Marcel found it difficult to swallow the meal, but he was in greater dread of the "entertainment" he was sure Mel had in store for the party after the banquet.

He was not mistaken. As dinner drew to an end, Mel announced that they would shortly reconvene down by the lakeside. Since the theme of the weekend was *environmental*, he declaimed, they were going to engage in a *pagan* celebration. Looking around the dining hall, he quizzed his colleagues about the significance of the day's date: 30 April.

"The eve of May Day," someone ventured.

"And of the first day of spring," another obliged.

"And," Mel continued, without waiting for any more suggestions, "the night of Beltane, the ancient Celtic fertility festival! I have invited a whole coven of witches to the Lodge tonight," he exclaimed exultantly, "to initiate us into the sacred mysteries of Beltane!" A roar of laughter and approval erupted around the room as Mel stepped down, ushering his guests out to a convoy of waiting minivans.

Long before the party arrived at the lake, Marcel could see in the darkness a huge bonfire lighting up a sweep of lawn that descended to the water's edge. A hush fell over the men as they disembarked. Around the fire, a group of naked young women stood in a circle. Completely covering the head of each was a large bird mask. There were ducks, geese, ibis, herons, grebes, crakes and cranes. The bird heads were larger-than-life, out of proportion to the girl's bodies, like the figures of animal-headed gods in ancient Egyptian papyruses or the bird-headed goddesses of Palaeolithic cave art. As the men walked slowly, slightly awed, down toward the lake, the girls began to dance in a circle. They danced gracefully, in an archaic style, emitting fluting calls, like the legendary wail of the loon. Marcel was spellbound in spite of himself. In the firelight, with the sheen of a wide expanse of water in the background, the spectacle was one of haunting and erotic beauty, the gentle, dark-eyed heads of the birds nodding slightly as the young women, their nubile bodies lustrous in the firelight, glided as if in flight.

Marcel stole a glance at Mel. The president was looking on with a small, satisfied smile, his eyes gleaming. The men hung back for quite some time watching while the girls continued to improvise their bird dance. Servants in rustic costume circulated amongst the men, dispensing drinks. After a while Marcel noticed that another, smaller fire had been prepared a little way up the slope, near the edge of a woodland. The girls gradually spiralled away from the bonfire and formed another circle around the smaller fire, beckoning the men to join them. Marcel saw cakes toasting in the embers of the fire. Mel announced that the girls were now going to initiate the guests in a traditional manner. Into each of these cakes—oatcakes, as it happened—a piece of paper with the ritual name of one of the witches had been baked. When the cakes were ready, the men would, one by one, take a cake from the fire, eat it, and call out the girl whose name he found inside the cake. He would then have to leap the flames to reach his allotted partner who would be waiting for him on the far side of the fire. If he succeeded, she would lead him away for a secret initiation in the woods.

The men gathered eagerly on one side of the fire, while the young women, their heads still hidden inside the bird masks, draped themselves over a blanket of petals and soft foliage on the other side. While the group waited for the cakes to toast, tension mounted. A quartet of medieval musicians materialized and began to play while the girls continued to hum and the men watched and drank. Eventually the cakes were ready and the guests took it in turns to select and eat one. It took no great effort to leap the flames, even in quite an advanced state of inebriation, and soon there were men lurching off in all directions into the woods with the girls whose lot had fallen to them. *So this is it*, thought Marcel, who had not yet taken his turn to select a cake. He had wanted to retreat but the scene had been so mesmerizing he had not been able to disengage. Now however—it was clear— the debauchery was about to begin. The men were drunk. The birds' heads would soon be cast aside. The beauty had been nothing but a mockery, a prelude to the desecration that was evidently to come. He was starting to fathom how Mel's sardonic mind worked. Stepping back into the shadows, he tried to slip off towards the vehicles. He had not gone far however before, with an anguished cry, a young girl, still wearing a duck's head, came running after him. She was brandishing a cake in her hand. He saw that she was the last. She had spied him attempting to escape. Now she seized his hand and, grasping it tightly, led him determinedly up to the woods.

Once amongst the trees, the girl drew Marcel to a secluded spot screened by brush that she had prepared earlier in the day. She turned to face him now, and slowly removing the duck head and shaking out her blonde hair, took his hand again and unceremoniously pressed it between her legs. He could only just see her face in the darkness, but she was young and very pretty in a truculent way. Obviously anxious that he might try to escape again, she was not wasting any time! He almost laughed. This was a twist on Leda and the swan!

With his usual composure, though, he merely asked, "Why are you women doing this? Are you really Wiccans?"

"I don't even know what a Wiccan is," the girl replied in a low voice. "We're sex workers, of course. We do whatever the client wants. Like suffocating inside this fucking mask," she added irritably. Marcel recoiled. He extricated himself hastily from her grip.

"You're pretty, but I've got to go."

The girl tried to detain him.

"I could lose my job if I don't please the client," she confessed urgently, with a muffled wail. "I'm on probation as it is!"

Marcel stumbled out of the bushes, astounded to hear the girl whispering a stream of obscenities and curses as he departed.

Shaken by the discordant elements of the evening and dismayed at having fallen for Mel's manipulations, Marcel decided to make his own way back to the lodge. Finding the road and following it up to the house, which would undoubtedly be well-lit, could not be so difficult. But the night was dark, and away from the festivities he could barely see at all. He had emerged from a different part of the woods than the part by which he had entered, and neither the bonfire nor the glint of the waiting vans was any longer visible. From the raucous sounds he could hear behind him however, an orgy seemed to be in full swing.

A feeling of dampness and the cold smell of water told him he was still close to the lake's edge, or at least to one of the adjoining swamps. Soft birdcalls wafted in from the water, and an owl could be heard making its rounds. Now, as if to derange his senses further, a light mist was rolling off the wetlands. Marcel walked, preferring to be lost than to return to the revels. He had already reached for his phone, but then remembered he had left it at the lodge. A sense of bleakness enveloped him. How did he come to be here? What was the path that had led to such a place of limbo, such a state of being nowhere at all? How had he found himself in such execrable company? What was the marriage to Mirielle worth if this was its cost? Why had he been prepared to sacrifice Ardea—and even his lion cub, Guri—at that tawdry altar? How and when had he so patently lost his way? The sounds of the party had been swallowed up in the silence of mist. His smart casual clothes were damp and the balminess of early spring had given way to a chill that seemed to have blown in from the depths of winter. Marcel was shivering. In the mist it was impossible to orient himself. He tried to follow upward gradients but kept finding himself on downward slopes again. Eventually, starting to tire, he realized he might just have to sit the night out until the orgy was finished and a search party was sent to rescue him.

Not that there was anywhere to sit. The ground underfoot was unstable, soggy. As he was hugging himself and rubbing his arms for warmth, wondering what to do next, a light came into view, glimmering feebly through layers of mist. Marcel knew there was a gamekeeper's cottage somewhere on the estate. Perhaps this was its porch light? He started off in its direction. But the ground became boggier and soon there was water squelching in his shoes. He realized he had strayed into a marsh. Truly alarmed at last, aware that he might wander into ever more treacherous terrain, Marcel tried to retrace his steps. But something caught his foot. He tripped, falling facedown into a rank pool. Gingerly raising himself, covered with mud and slime, he looked for the light again but it was gone. He had tumbled at an awkward angle, twisting his shoulder and side. Exploring with his hands, he discovered a rotting stump that must have been the cause of his fall. He leaned cautiously against it, clasping his shoulder.

Perhaps this is how it will end, he thought forlornly. *Here. Alone. In this extremity of isolation.* A powerful sense of déjà vu gripped him. Hadn't he been in this nightmare before? Often. Always? *Hello darkness, my old friend.* He eased his head back, closed his eyes and tried to conjure his life, but it had receded and contracted, all the colour and glitter reduced to a distant bubble. Even Mirielle's face was indistinct, far off, as if he had never properly looked at her at all. If this was the end, where were his memories? There were only charades, scenes from a movie, different movies. His mother was there though, still immediate, in endless close-up. His beautiful, bohemian, vain and self-absorbed mother. He groaned inwardly at the thought of her. Familiar images flitted through his mind. Of her painting half-naked upstairs in her studio. Of her draped like a pagan goddess around their marble apartment, trailing wraps and robes, while servants looked after him. How could the flesh of one small, female creature and one pair of lambent eyes possess such a pervasive charge, such inexhaustible allure? Their home was steeped in it. He and his father had struggled to escape it. A boy is supposed to wish his father dead, Marcel reflected bitterly, but in his case how far from the truth that was. It was he himself who had been sacrificed on the altar of his mother's beauty, condemned to re-enact that sacrifice on others, over and over and over, without relief. It seemed to him now that he had been snared in the mystique of those wraps and robes his entire life, mesmerized, on a treadmill of illusory desires, barely aware of the world around him.

But now, now, reality had caught up with him. *This* was reality, this cold—he felt mud trickling down the inside of his shirt—this dull pain, this wetness, this nothingness, this inevitability. After a lifetime of obliviousness towards it, reality was now reduced for him to bruteness. *If this is the end, bring it on*, he thought harshly. Better bruteness than being snared forever in the miasma of those stupid robes, and all the stupid fantasies and false ambitions that had emanated from them. Where was his grief in the face of such futility? His anger? Regret? Self-pity? Recrimination? There was no emotion. Just the ache in his shoulder, the chatter of his teeth, a desolation as vast and cold as outer space, and a mental shudder at the thought of Mel.

Opening his eyes however, Marcel now caught the glimmer of another light. It seemed no bigger than a lantern, though not too distant. With an effort, he sat up. Perhaps it was a servant sent to search for him? Painfully he stood and managed some stumbling steps towards it, calling out. His call was met with silence. Again he called, more loudly, with just the hint of a sob in his voice. Clasping his shoulder he started limping through reeds that were up to his knees, trying to avoid the snags that littered the marsh. The light receded, but it was joined now by others, four or five of them, bobbing and zigzagging exactly as if they had been lanterns carried by a search party—or by the spirits to whose rule these marshlands perhaps reverted at night. It was a beautiful and ethereal spectacle in the half-mist, Marcel noted, though he was in no condition to appreciate it. He called out again, without conviction. Dimly he recollected that he had heard of this phenomenon. At once it dawned on him. "Will o'the wisps!" he exclaimed. The *ignis fatuus*...marsh gas. Conjured, he had no doubt, to lead him to his doom!

At a standstill now, enclosed in dark mist, Marcel started

to shiver in earnest, uncontrollably. His core heat was draining abruptly out of his body. At a total loss, he wavered on his feet, scarcely able to remain upright. At the very same moment however he registered a strange sound. In the middle distance. Was it a frog? It had a static, almost electronic timbre, too forceful for a frog's call. Marcel's ears strained. The only thing to which he could compare it was the ma-ma-ma of an old-fashioned doll when one turned it over. But then the realization struck him: it must be a deer! Not that he knew anything at all about deer, but what else could it be? Had it responded to his own gut cry? In any case, if a deer it was then it must be on dry ground. With a surge of strength he turned and started limping in the direction from whence the sound had come. He neither looked back nor paused, but ploughed forward resolutely. Soon the ground began to rise slightly, and he was encouraged. Perhaps he had regained the slope that led up to the road. This did indeed prove to be the case. He found himself ascending, and the mist began to clear. By starlight he could see he was in parkland dotted with copses and edged with woods, and his step quickened. Before too long his feet hit tarmac. He had found the road! Even if he set off in the wrong direction, the road would take him down to the entrance gate, from whence he would only have to retrace his steps and continue walking to reach the lodge. He did not choose the wrong direction however, and an uncomfortable thirty-minute march at last brought the blaze of the lodge into view. A few people were standing in the reception area, but Marcel found a side entrance and slipped up to his room, his mortification mercifully unwitnessed.

After a hot shower, the pain in Marcel's shoulder eased. He longed to leave the lodge, but, shaken by the night's events, was uncertain. Should he stand his ground? What ground? What was his ground? He felt unready to make decisions that might alter his life. His life. What was his life? He turned away with pain from the thought. There would be time to reflect in due course.

The following morning, scrubbed and freshly attired, he

descended to breakfast. In the dining room he was met by only Mel, Darian and Wilber. Mel, who had just come in from his usual gruelling morning run and was towelling his torso, beamed at Marcel but made no reference to the previous evening.

"Where are the others," Marcel asked.

"I've organized something very special for today," Mel replied. "We'll be going on an excursion, and it will be just a select group—he gestured around the table. We drive to the launch immediately after breakfast."

Marcel prickled with dread but was still irresolute.

"What kind of excursion," he ventured.

Mel laughed. "An *environmental* excursion, of course," he returned with mock geniality. "I've organized it especially for you."

After breakfast the four men boarded a mini-bus with a load of gear—wet suits, Marcel noticed, as well as waders and weapons. They drove for half an hour to a private jetty in a swampy area that to Marcel was beginning to look disturbingly familiar. He suspected they were in the hinterland of the Onaway estuary. A motor launch awaited them, and they loaded it not only with gear but a small dinghy. For half an hour they motored along a deep channel until, sure enough, mangroves started to appear. When the mangroves thickened and the channel petered out, they transferred to the dinghy. With a maritime GPS system, Wilber navigated through heavy mangrove forest. Marcel was aware of the same dreamy mood he had experienced with Ardea in this phantasmagorical setting, but the atmosphere in the group was tense, leaving no room for mystical communion.

Mel was low-key. Finally he commented to the other two men that they could thank Marcel for this adventure. It was Marcel, he explained, who had discovered, via undercover activities—here he smiled at Marcel—the presence of great white herons in the estuary.

"Ah," Marcel conceded, "but unfortunately my espionage skills were not up to finding the actual location of the nest site—the information that is really critical to the development."

"Oh," Mel demurred, with a dismissive gesture. "An un-important detail. The real achievement was warning us of the presence of the species. Locating the nesting site has been a simple operation. I employed our own university biologists to do an aerial survey. Wilber has the GPS of the colony in his hands this very moment."

Marcel's sense of grim inevitability deepened. He noticed that the guns in the back of the dinghy were sheathed in wa-ter-tight sleeves. Wilber signalled that they were now not far from their destination and it would soon be time to change into their wet suits.

When they came to a dense wall of mangrove, Darian tied up the dinghy and the four men clambered, wet-suited and begoggled, into the water, each of them, bar Marcel, carrying a gun sleeve. Darian led them through the thicket, wading chest-deep till at length they came to shallower waters on the far side. Marcel saw they were in the precincts of a large, fully enclosed pool. As the other men unsheathed their weapons, he observed that the pool was refuge for a rich variety of bird life. Moreover, immediately visible, presiding over the tran-quil scene, was the stately figure of a great white heron, high in the upper branches of the tallest stag tree. With an alacrity that took Marcel unawares, leaving him no chance to collect his wits or even look around, Darian and Wilber were already silently taking aim. There was a momentary pause before Mel, standing stock still, murmured "Fire!"

At that very moment, Marcel caught sight of other figures on the far side of the pool. Young people. He recognized them at once. They were wearing the colours of Ardea's group, Sea Watch. Students! Reclining on a raft tethered to the mangroves' edge but rising to their knees in alarm as they became aware of the intrusion. Time slowed to freeze-frames for Marcel as he registered the situation. Before he could speak, the guns had fired. But the white heron, also alerted to the disturbance at the thicket's edge, had already swooped from the tree. Keeping it in their sights, the men continued to fire. The three students, still indistinct figures in the play of reflected light and shade and sheets of dazzle, dived into the water, screaming, attempting to deflect the shooters' attention. Confused, and in a reflex reaction, the men strafed the pool with their automatic weapons, determined not to miss their target. In disbelief, Marcel saw the water explode into sheets of spray; when it flattened out again there was total silence and the students had vanished. Only the shattered body of the white heron was visible on the surface of the water, while to either side of it a few limp flaps marked the dying struggles of other water birds. Mel was also staring at the scene in disbelief. "Morons!" he hissed at Darian and Wilber from between clenched teeth, jabbing the air with his fist.

Thrashing clumsily now in their hurry, the men waded around the edge of the pool to where the young people had disappeared. It did not take them long to locate the bodies in brackish shallows. They dragged them onto a sand bar close to where the raft was moored. As Darian turned the bodies over, Marcel and Mel saw simultaneously that one of the students was Guri. Staring grimly at Marcel, Mel stated in a flat and threatening voice, "There's been a hunting accident."

As he spoke, another white heron appeared overhead. Without waiting for orders, Wilber swiftly took aim and again fired. The bird dropped straight into the water in front of them. Though wounded, it was clearly not yet dead. Impulsively, Marcel plunged out to save it. "Finish it off," barked Mel, his face dark and taut. Wilber hesitated, as Marcel was in the way. Marcel, up to his waist in water, seized the bird and gathered it to him. It struggled only slightly. He turned to face the men. If they fired at the bird they would shoot him through the chest. Wilber glanced at Mel, who said nothing, though his eyes bulged. There was a long pause. Then Mel muttered, turning away and kicking viciously at the shattered body of a cormorant that had washed up to shore, "He's as dead as this duck anyway now he's joined the loon brigade." He repeated to Darian in a louder voice, "There's been a hunting accident. Call the police." As the three men began to wade back towards the point where they could navigate through the thicket to the dinghy, Mel added, "Don't dial 911." He yanked the phone from Darian's hand

and keyed a number into it himself. None of the men looked back at Marcel.

Marcel had not moved. The white heron had ceased struggling and was limp. Its great wings were open against his torso, its neck looped, its head cradled on his shoulder. Blood was reddening the water in which he stood. His eyes, squeezed shut, streamed, whether with tears or brine he could not tell. He bowed his head then touched his cheek to the downy curve of the bird's breast. A few white feathers had wafted into the water around him. Stunned though he was at the sudden and shocking turn of events, raw energy and anger were coursing through him. Opening his eyes, he stared at Mel's retreating back, muttering, between gritted teeth, *over my dead body.* Was he speaking for the heron or of his own defiance? He did not know. All he knew was that everything had, in an instant, irrevocably shifted. From here on, it would all be different; nothing was foreseeable. The men disappeared into the mangroves. The deserted pool, the thickets, the island, the heron's head on his shoulder came toward him in preternatural focus, as if he had stepped right through an invisible veil into close-up with actuality. From within the huge hush of horror, there was a nascent stirring of wonder. For one long, further moment, Marcel hugged the heron to his chest, breathing in its salty smell, flinching under its unexpected weight, not forgetting, from a rearmost recess of his mind, to marvel at the astonishing detail, the individual shafts and barbs, the intricate, alien forest of its feathers. Then he bore the body to the beach, and laying it tenderly at the water's edge, turned back to Guri.

Afterword

It is time to leave Marcel, abandoned there amongst the mangroves, still too stunned to register the sudden re-constellation that has taken place. He has fallen out of his old life and momentarily entered a new world, the real world. But will he stay to explore it, to make himself at home in it? He has met Ardea—one archetype has been introduced to another, as the earth-goddesses of the Mediterranean were once introduced to the sky-gods that swept down from the northern steppes. But will he and the Ardeans "inter-marry", will the stories cross-fertilize, as those of the earth-goddesses and sky-gods did in the ancient world? As storyteller, I do not yet know. The curtain has fallen on the narrative at this particular juncture and though I have, like Goethe, waited years for that curtain to rise, it has not done so. As I mentioned at the outset, I suspect that Goethe forced the issue with Faust. In desperation, at the very end of his life, he seems to have imposed an abrupt and discordant ending on a narrative that had not yet resolved its inner tensions. This was a dangerous last resort, for Faust was a figure with deep mythical or Dreaming underpinnings, and hence immense invocational power. To launch him, flawed, was to court incalculable consequences.

Our world is surely shaped as much by meaning as it is by technology and other forms of causality. Stories with roots in myth or Dreaming may perhaps be understood as narrative abstractions from the large-scale patterns of meaning shaping a given historical and environmental moment. In that sense, such stories capture truth. One *discovers* such truth, just as one discovers truths in science; one does not invent it. Since meanings unfold in accordance with their own inner logic moreover, stories prefigure possibilities, and, by revealing the inner shape of circumstances, usher us into the future. Stories with the depth or resonance of myth can, in other words, help us to steer our civilization.

But such stories are not oracles. They need to be mixed into the texture of the present, circulated, shared, given a chance to crystallize and re-align thought patterns, before their sequels come to the surface. Without knowing whether the tale of the encounter here told—between Faust and the Ardeans—will achieve any resonance at all, I feel obliged to open my authorial hand and let Ardea take flight, as the first part of a story whose second part may in due course be discovered by myself or other future tellers.

I do this on a day of high, unseasonal and threatening winds, my house, at the foot of its stone mountain, rocking on its stumps. It is a daunting environment in which to release a tiny, tender, fledgling story, but this new tempestuous climate is surely now the defining context for any and all transactions with the Dreaming.